Beneath the Stars

ASHLAND ROMANCE

Beneath the Stars

Copyright ©2025 by Dana-Susan Crews

Published by Ashland Ink Publishing
209 West 2nd Street #177
Fort Worth TX 76102
www.bellasteri.com

Published in the United States of America

ISBN: 978-1-963514-22-3 (hardback)
ISBN: 978-1-963514-21-6 (paperback)
ISBN: 978-1-963514-23-0 (e-book)

Beneath the Stars

DANA-SUSAN CREWS

ASHLAND ROMANCE

PREFACE
The Stars

The midnight sky is a velvet canvas, stitched with diamonds that flicker like secrets whispered from the heavens. Their brilliance pours over the world like liquid silver, washing the land in quiet magic. Each sparkle fills me with a breath of hope, a reminder that even in my heaviest storms and sweetest triumphs, I have always returned to their glow.

But the stars hide from the city, swallowed by neon signs, choked by smoke and restless noise. And maybe that's where I unraveled. When their light was stolen, my own flame faltered, and I stumbled blind in the shadows. Yet the stars, stubborn and eternal, never truly left. They waited, patient beacons, to guide me back. This is not just the tale of how I wandered into darkness when their shine dimmed within me. It is also the story of how their radiant fire rekindled my soul and led me home.

CHAPTER 1
Big City

At twenty-one, I traded the quiet harmony of a small town for the restless pulse of a big city. Just a month after graduating from college, an entire year ahead of schedule, I landed a job in the city's downtown, perched high above the streets on the thirtieth floor of a gleaming skyscraper. For a girl who had spent her whole life in a small town, the city was dizzying. I stumbled my way through unfamiliar streets, wrestled with parking garages, and tried to quiet my mind in a place where silence didn't seem to exist. Every task felt like a test. Could I adapt? Could I keep up? Could I learn to think in all this noise? I hadn't known it then, but each little challenge was the beginning of a battle I was determined to win.

My interview for this job took place on my college campus, another small town not far from home, so my first day on the job was also my first day in the office. My dad had helped me figure out where to live one week before I started the job.

We found a luxury apartment only a few blocks away from the office. Dad thought it felt safe. He was a good, old-fashioned country boy who struggled to see me move to such a big city, so finding this apartment complex was a godsend. It had a nice parking garage, and it was a very peaceful, quiet place, even though it was in the middle of downtown.

In just one whirlwind week, I mapped out my little corner of this vast city. I uncovered the nearest grocery store, tracked down a nearby Target, and even slipped into a nail salon where easy conversation and cheer filled the air like sunshine through a window. A surprisingly good hair salon appeared like a hidden gem. I discovered restaurants I had never heard of, and I learned that I like sushi. Still, despite the discoveries, I had exactly zero friends here. In a place pulsing with millions of lives, I felt invisible and alone. Back home, friendships sprouted naturally, woven through school halls, Sunday pews, and dusty football fields. But here? The city glittered, yet it felt like a glittering kind of loneliness, dazzling but empty, a crowd without a community.

Two days before I began my job, I returned from another trip to Target and bumped into one of my neighbors. Literally. I didn't see him because I had too many big bags in my hands, and he was walking out of the building while I was walking in. I apologized and said, "I'm so clumsy." He laughed and held the door for me so I could make it in. He also offered to help me get to my apartment, but I declined. He was tall and handsome. He had a square jaw and dark hair with a perfectly shaped beard. He had piercing green eyes and a big dimple on his cheek. I almost got awkward as he held the door, but I quickly pulled myself together and thanked him. Then I walked into my apartment and made a wish. "I wish to marry a man who looks just like him," I whispered. Since I've never really been one to care about appearances, the thought surprised me, and I couldn't help but laugh at myself for it.

I could have walked to work, but I wasn't about to risk the wind undoing my carefully styled hair. So, on my first day, I slid behind the wheel, convinced I'd left with plenty of time to spare. Another hard truth about city life? Driving can take longer than walking. Still, I made it, just in time.

The reception area of my new office felt warm the moment I stepped inside, thanks to Mary, a cheerful, silver-haired woman who greeted me as though she'd been expecting me. Without a single word of introduction, she knew exactly who I was. She proudly explained that she was the office manager and had kept things running smoothly there for nearly twelve years. She led me through a maze of cubicles until we stopped at mine, right in the middle of the bustling room. Waiting on my desk was a welcome bag of "goodies," as Mary called them, including my temporary work badge, a handful of office supplies, and even some candy to sweeten my first day. She mentioned we'd head down later for my photo so I could get a permanent badge. Before leaving me to settle in, Mary introduced me to Katie and James, my new neighbors in the sea of cubicles.

Katie was a tiny young woman in her mid-twenties with long blonde hair and what appeared to be enhanced breasts, the kind I had only ever seen in the movies. She was what you would describe as "bubbly" and cute. Immediately, she wanted to arrange coffee and lunch dates with me, and she promised to show me where all the "most fabulous" places were to eat and get iced coffee, and go out dancing. I felt overwhelmed.

James was around his late twenties or early thirties. He was a little overweight and beginning to go bald. He wore glasses and looked older than his age. I noticed he was wearing a wedding band. He wasn't as talkative as Katie, but he was friendly and kind and told me he would happily join Katie and me for lunch dates. He mentioned that he would be on vacation all the following week as his wife's family had a reunion out of town.

I sat at my desk and put in my earbuds to begin my many hours of onboarding. My anxiety from the morning began to fade, and I was one of those weirdos who actually enjoyed the goofy videos during my training. I think I might have even laughed out loud at one of them. That's a bit embarrassing.

An hour into my training, my new boss came to greet me. Betty McDonald was the accounting supervisor, so she was in charge of the entire accounting team I was on. That included me, James, Katie, and three other people I had yet to meet. Betty apologized for not greeting me when I arrived. She told me that her two-year-old had a fever that morning and that she had to arrange for her mother-in-law to come over to babysit her all day. I felt so sorry for her that she had to be at work with a sick toddler at home, and I thought to myself, "I hope that when I have children, I can be at home with them instead of here." I was also told that Betty and the team would be taking me to lunch and that we would be leaving at 11:45 to head to a place called Oskar's, which was apparently a great place to order a steak salad.

My morning flew by as I did my onboarding videos, and I got my photo taken for my badge. I texted my dad to let him know how I was doing. He had begged me the night before to keep him updated. I did not want to disappoint him. I knew he was a laid-back, easy-going man most of the time, but when it came to me, he tended to worry. He replied to my text immediately with a heart emoji and an "I love you, Sweetie." Dad. He's had a lot of big burdens to bear. Knowing he was all alone in a big house far away made me sad, but I also knew he would throw himself into his many projects on the ranch and spend lots of time in town with his group of friends. He had many friends in our hometown, and his life was good.

Katie came to my desk several times that morning to "check" on me. Each time, she stayed for a while and filled me in on all the happenings in town. She told me about some of the clubs where she and her friends liked to dance and about the cool concerts and sporting events. She informed me that our company often gave tickets to football or baseball games to the employees. I learned that she was newly single, having just recently broken up with her boyfriend of two years, and that he was a "total douche." She made sure to exchange phone numbers with me so she could invite me out with her friends. I didn't want to give her my number. I was afraid I would be a party pooper of sorts. I do not like big crowds or meeting new people. I am fairly shy, an introvert who wants the companionship of a small group. But I was new in town, and I wasn't about to turn down social interaction when I was all alone.

Lunch time rolled around, and Betty and my new coworkers all walked to Oskar's, a really nice restaurant two blocks away and packed with people. I met the others on my team. They included Dale, a mid-thirties dad to a baby and a four-year-old, both boys. He was married to a teacher who was at home working on lesson plans for the upcoming school year, which was only two weeks away from beginning. There was Carol, a forty-year-old divorced mom of a twelve-year-old daughter who was a volleyball player. And then there was Paul, a volunteer youth minister at a local church. He was twenty-eight years old, single, and average-looking at best. He was in good shape, though. It was obvious he spent some time at the gym. The way he smiled at me made me think, "he's into me." I never think like that. I never notice anyone noticing me at all. Why Paul? There was just a sparkle in his eyes. He had deep, dark blue eyes, and they were his best feature. At lunch, he sat next to me and dominated my attention. He was outgoing. He very much enjoyed talking about his activities, many of which revolved around his church. Of course, he invited me to "check it out."

The afternoon stretched on like a long shadow, slow and heavy. Fatigue clung to me. I hadn't slept well in days, not since the move, and my body felt as though it had been running on borrowed energy. By the time I left work, a strange current ran through me, a tingle of uncertainty, almost like standing at the edge of a cliff and wondering if I had really chosen the right path. I had accepted this job because I believed in the possibility of a new beginning, a chance to rebuild myself in a city that vibrated with opportunity. I wanted to prove that I could step into adulthood on my own terms, but right then, all I could feel was exhaustion pressing against my bones.

I said goodbye to my new coworkers, faces still unfamiliar, voices not yet woven into the fabric of my life, and stepped into the parking garage. Relief washed over me when I remembered I had groceries waiting at home. Nothing fancy, just the promise of a sandwich and the comfort of mindless television before surrendering to sleep.

That night, as I slipped into bed, the hum of the city beyond my window felt oddly comforting. I closed my eyes and whispered a quiet prayer of gratitude for making it through day one of this new job, and for surviving the first week of my life here. I asked God for guidance, for protection, for courage to keep going. And then, as though my body finally trusted that it was safe, I drifted into the deepest sleep I'd had in weeks, cocooned in the hope that maybe, just maybe, I was where I was meant to be.

Crews

CHAPTER 2
Here I Come, Future

One week at the new job had vanished in a blur, and suddenly it was Friday, the official end of onboarding. The office was unusually quiet. Most of my coworkers were already enjoying their long weekend. Only Katie and I remained, part of the rotation that ensured at least two people held down the fort on Fridays. We were on the 9/80 schedule, which meant longer days but the sweet reward of every other Friday off. I didn't mind the trade-off. The long hours kept me busy, and the bonus days gave me time to breathe, catch up on errands, or, as my dad reminded me, take long weekends to visit home.

By mid-afternoon, the quiet hum of the office was suddenly broken when Katie appeared at my cubicle, practically bouncing. "Time to go, Chica!" she squealed. I remember being amused by her use of the Spanish word for girl. It didn't take long to realize this was simply Katie's way. She called all her girlfriends "chica," whether on the phone or chatting across the office. It wasn't about Spanish because she didn't speak it. It was just part of her playful vocabulary, a patchwork of Spanish, English, borrowed phrases from various languages, and her own invented expressions.

That night, she had invited me to join her friends at a club. A part of me knew it would be smart to go, to meet new people, to say yes. But the week had drained me, and what I wanted more than anything was pajamas, a couch, and the mindless comfort of binge-watching *Gilmore Girls*. So, I smiled and told her I already had plans, asking her to keep me in the loop for next time. The truth was, I didn't want to risk losing the invitation altogether. Katie's social calendar was endless. Weekends, weeknights, sometimes both. She was, without question, a party girl. Or should I say "party chica?"

As I made it out of the building and into the parking garage, I nearly collapsed in exhaustion on my steering wheel. It had been a good week. I had learned a lot about my position. I had gone to lunch or coffee almost every day with Katie and James. And twice, Paul joined us. Both of those times, it seemed like he and Katie were competing for who could talk the most.

Thursday, as he was packing up to leave, Paul invited me to attend his church on Sunday. He told me what time to be there and where to meet him so he could introduce me to the young adults in the Sunday morning Bible study. I agreed to go, worried he would think that I wanted a relationship with him, but also realizing that a Bible study would probably be way better for my social life than going to clubs with Katie.

So, now my only weekend obligation was church on

Sunday. I could go home and not think for a while. As I pulled away from work, I felt a cold wind hit my face, and the world seemed to go dark for an entire second. Was that a weird daydream of sorts? I shrugged it off and got home. I was glad I had planned ahead and had ordered an extra meal from the Chinese place down the street on Wednesday night. I put on my pajamas, heated up my fried rice and egg rolls, opened up my Netflix to season one, episode one of *Gilmore Girls*, and began my easy, happy weekend.

Thirty minutes later, I received a call from my dad's neighbor, Mrs. Dubbs. Why would she be calling me? "Hello," I said in a shocked voice.

"Callie, Dear," she began with a tearful crackle, "I'm afraid I have some bad news."

Life can change in an instant. One minute, you are blissfully binge-watching your favorite show, and the next, you enter a torment you could not imagine. As I listened to Mrs. Dubbs tell me that my dad had been hauled away in an ambulance and that his heart was not beating, I knew he was gone. She offered "hope" as she said the paramedics had been working on him. But I knew. You see, that cold darkness I had felt as I left the parking garage was my dad leaving the world. It was not my first experience with that feeling. Later, I would learn that that had been the exact moment when his heart failed.

I was glad I had my boss's phone number. I left her a voicemail letting her know about my dad and telling her I would not be at work on Monday. It is so strange to start a job and only be there one week before already taking time off.

The drive home was excruciating. My eyes were filled with tears, and my heart wanted to leap from my chest. What was in reality only a five-hour journey felt like a five-day journey. Twice, I pulled over to weep. By the time I arrived at the hospital, they had already called the time of death, and I walked alone into a hospital room to see my dad lying on a gurney, dead.

I held his hand. I kissed his cheek. I whispered in his ear that I loved him. He wasn't there, though. I didn't feel him there. He was in heaven, reunited with my mom and brother. He was happy and free. But I was alone. My entire family was gone. They had left me here in this world to live out the rest of my days without them. It was all too much to bear.

Almost ten years before, when I was 12 years old, my mom and my 15-year-old brother Simon were killed in a car accident on the way home from his taekwondo practice. My mom had swerved to miss a tire in the road and hit a patch of ice. The first responders all told my dad that they had died instantly without pain. I always wondered how they knew that. Maybe they just say things like that to bring a bit of comfort in an otherwise tragic situation.

Neither my dad nor I had ever truly recovered from the accident. There would always be two big holes in our hearts. But my dad did everything in his power to give me the best life possible. He took on the role of mom and dad. He was at every sports event and every school awards ceremony. He gave of himself even when there wasn't much of him left to give. I think at night, he cried. But with me, he smiled. He wanted my life to be good. In the moment I had alone with his body in the hospital, I hoped that he knew he was successful, that my life had been a good one because he had been a good dad. My dear dad's heart just couldn't stand having those holes in it any longer. And I was five hours away. He felt isolated, and I guess he gave in to the desire to let go.

I kissed his cheek once more before walking out into the hall. By now, there were many friends and neighbors congregated and crying. They were hugging each other and me. Many tears flowed in the halls of that hospital, and as the sun rose the next day, I had work to do.

My dad's mom was still alive, but all of my other grandparents were in heaven. Grandma and I cried many times as we made funeral arrangements. I wished we could just have a small, intimate service, but Grandma wanted everyone to be there. She lived in a tiny apartment in town. She contacted the pastor of our church to officiate. Dad was well-known in town, so it was obvious that the church would be packed. I was having flashbacks to my mom and brother's funeral. I was struggling to breathe. I was struggling to eat. But I kept hearing my dad's voice saying, "Sweetie, you gotta stay strong."

On Monday, my boss called to check on me. She told me not to worry at all about how long I was out, to take all the time I needed. I'd only been there a week, but they sent flowers to the service. The funeral was Wednesday. It was packed. I was overwhelmed, feeling the pressure to greet everyone when all I wanted to do was be alone with my grief.

Then, I was finally alone. Grandma had stayed with me those first few nights, but I told her I was fine now and that I just needed some time alone at home. I sat on the big front porch overlooking the pasture. A gentle breeze brushed through my hair, and suddenly the sky was filled with bright stars. I found myself jealous of my parents and brother. They were up there with the stars. They were walking along golden streets in a perfect and peaceful place, while I was left in a broken world filled with sorrow.

There would be a lot of work to do over the next few weeks, but I decided that night that I would return to the city and my job on Monday. My dad would have wanted me to do that. And I had enough experience with grief to know that it can own you if you let it. I would go to my grave mourning the loss, but I would not let the grief own me.

Grandma's arms clung to me, her embrace trembling as I loaded the last of my things into the car. I could feel the ache in her chest as much as my own. Hers was a heart weathered by too much loss. Her husband had died many years before. Then she lost her daughter-in-law and her grandson. And now her son. My uncle had come from far across state lines, staying here in town to shoulder the weight of details I was too young and too raw to carry alone. My father had left me everything. His 1,000-acre ranch, his belongings, and all his money. Uncle Jeremy, his brother, promised to help me gather it into order, to place it safely in accounts, and to sell the land that was too much for me to tend. Letting go of the ranch felt like letting go of him, yet we all knew I could not keep it. And so, with Grandma's quiet sorrow and my uncle's steady hand, the decision was made.

Gravel whispered beneath my tires as I left the warmth of my childhood home, dust rising like ghosts of yesterday. At twenty-one, I was no longer the girl sipping icy lemonade on the wide porch, laughter spilling into the summer air beside my dad. That chapter had closed with the creak of the screen door, and ahead stretched the vast, trembling unknown of the future. Fear fluttered like a wild bird in my chest, but I carried my dad's lesson etched into my bones: "Meet fear eye to eye, and do not flinch."

So I leaned into the horizon, heart open, whispering, "Here I come, Future!"

Crews

CHAPTER 3
Daniel

Returning to work felt less awkward for me than for everyone else. My coworkers, who had only just met me, seemed suddenly unsure of their behavior in front of me. Their silence wasn't unkind, just clumsy, as though they didn't know which words were safe to use, or whether words could possibly be enough. It would fall to me, I realized, to ease them into something resembling normal.

So I chose Katie and James as my anchors. On my first morning back, I broke the silence.

"I just want you both to know that I'm going to be fine," I told them, steadying my own voice. I even added a small invitation, suggesting we grab coffee or lunch soon.

Katie, warm-hearted and earnest, wrapped me in a quick hug. She confessed that she had lost a cousin to childhood cancer many years ago, her way of offering me a bridge into her own understanding of grief. It was compassionate, and I appreciated her effort. James, quieter, simply smiled and touched my shoulder. "I'm sorry for your loss," he said. Nothing more, and somehow, that simplicity carried its own weight.

The truth was, what could anyone say? They didn't know about my mom and brother, gone years ago. Over coffee a few days later, Katie asked about my family, and I told her that my dad had been my only one left, that the others had been taken long before. The air grew heavy in an instant, laden with a silence that was more than uncomfortable. It was sorrowful, searching, wordless.

For a moment, I felt exposed, as if my life was too jagged, too full of loss, to sit politely at a café table. Embarrassment prickled in me, and I feared the kind of pity that builds walls instead of bridges. So I smiled, steady and bright, and reassured them both. I told them I was fine, that I had plenty of friends and extended family back home. I repeated it, almost like a charm against grief. *I'm fine. I'm fine.*

But I wasn't fine. I was isolated. I was lost. I was grief-stricken. I wanted to talk to my dad. Paul came to chat with me a few times that week, mostly about work-related things and to once again invite me to his church. I told him that I would definitely go on Sunday morning.

My weekend was quiet. I sat on my couch and cried. I talked to my grandma on the phone. I forced myself to eat. I looked up at God and asked Him to show me a purpose for my life. It was excruciating trying to get out of bed and get dressed on Sunday morning. But I had promised Paul and myself that I would go to church.

I arrived and walked into the front doors, and turned left, where there was a coffee bar. Paul had told me to meet him there. There were many young adults congregating in this area. When Paul walked up, he greeted me with a small hug and then began introducing me to some of the others there.

Jackie was a tall, beautiful brunette with round cheeks and piercing brown eyes. I felt an instant connection to her. She was not overly outgoing, but kind and welcoming. There was a calm, peacefulness about her. Stephanie was a loud and very funny redhead who was the type to say whatever she was thinking without actually thinking about whether she should say it. Todd was a bit of a nerdy type who was wearing a Star Wars shirt. He was smart and seemed to be very friendly, and I liked that he was also obviously proud of his nerdiness. Then there was Daniel. He was not the most handsome guy I had ever met, just average, really. He was average in height, average in attractiveness, and even average in physical fitness. But I felt a surge run through my body when he shook my hand. It was obvious he felt it, too.

I did not know it at the time, but this was my new group. This was my "family" in my new city, in my new life. Jackie, Stephanie, Todd, Daniel, and me. We would soon develop a bond. Paul seemed to grasp that I had no interest in him romantically, and before long, he and I only talked at work when we were in a meeting together or working on a group project.

As days turned to weeks and then to months, I began to feel more at home in my new city. My small group of church friends was my everything. We got together every weekend and many times throughout the week. I joined the church softball team with them. We played every Tuesday night, and then we'd go grab burgers and stay out way too late for a work night. Jackie and I grew especially close, and soon, I considered her my best friend. In many ways, she was like a sister. I had always wished for a sister, and now I had one. Just a couple of months before I had moved to town, Jackie's younger sister had gotten married. Jackie was twenty-seven years old and feeling very alone. All she had ever longed for was marriage and a family of her own, yet the right man had never crossed her path. When her younger sister, barely twenty-four, walked down the aisle, envy burned like salt in an open wound.

It was now October, and the crispy air and my new family of five brought a fresh sense of joy my way. Back home, my uncle had sold the ranch to a young man who had dreamed of starting his own cattle ranch. According to my grandma, he was a true gentleman who reminded her of my dad when he was younger. This gave her much-needed peace that my dad's place would be cherished and treated well.

Stephanie had arranged for our group to go on a haunted hay ride, which happened to coincide with my twenty-second birthday. We met for dinner and then headed to the event, where we huddled together on the trailer covered in warm blankets and sipping hot chocolate. My friends had pitched in to buy me a framed print of the skyline of my new city. I loved it.

Over the months, Daniel had flirted with me a lot, but he had yet to ask me on a date. Sometimes, I could tell that Todd seemed to have a crush on me, too. But Todd and I only ever really talked about video games and Star Wars. Stephanie would often behave like she had a crush on Todd, but she promised Jackie and me that she only wanted to be his friend. Stephanie was the oldest of us all. At thirty, she was beginning to think she would never get married. She thought of herself as "fat," even though I would just say she was curvy. Sometimes I thought she was so loud and constantly telling jokes because she was deeply insecure. I loved Stephanie and wished she could find her "Mr. Right." I also wished she knew how adorable she was.

On the hay ride, Daniel and I shared a blanket. As the night got darker and the ride got scarier, he grabbed my hand in what seemed like an accident, but he didn't let go. Neither did I. I felt that surge again, the one I had felt the morning we met. I had dated some in high school and college, but I had never truly been in a long, committed relationship. I was, after all, only twenty-two. Daniel was twenty-nine. He had been engaged before. When he was twenty-three, he was engaged to his college girlfriend. Only two months into their engagement, she broke up with him, saying that she just wasn't ready to get married. One year later, she walked down the aisle to marry one of his college roommates. Daniel was crushed. He told me that she was "crazy" and that his heart had been so shattered that he didn't think he would ever love again.

When I look back at this now, I wonder about her. Was she really crazy? Or was she wise and escaping something that would destroy her? But that night, on that hay ride, under the blanket, we held hands. And I tingled all over.

Daniel called me the next morning and asked if I would go to dinner with him. As soon as I got off the phone, I called Jackie. She came to help me pick out an outfit. I did not expect her to be as excited about this dinner date as she was.

She told me that she had secretly hoped that Daniel and I would get together all along. That truly surprised me because secretly, I wondered if Jackie liked Daniel. Every so often, I'd catch her watching him, her gaze lingering a beat too long, as if she were tracing some unspoken thought across his face. The instant she realized she'd been caught, she'd snap her attention elsewhere, a little too quickly, as though she could erase the moment. Still, when she burst with delight over the news of my date with him, her joy so effortless, so convincing, I pushed aside my suspicions. Surely I had just imagined it.

I stood before the mirror, smoothing the skirt of my dress and glancing down at my sneakers, the playful balance between casual and sweet. My blonde hair was pulled back neatly, and a fresh swipe of pink lipstick brightened my smile. What startled me most wasn't the reflection itself, but the flutter in my chest, the unexpected thrill of anticipation. I hadn't realized, until this moment, that my feelings for Daniel had slipped quietly into something romantic. Now, with my heart racing, I felt like a giddy schoolgirl stepping into her very first date.

Daniel pulled up in front of my apartment and sent a quick text, "I'm here." I snatched my small purse, heart fluttering, and hurried downstairs, a laugh almost catching in my throat. When I stepped outside, he was waiting by the car, and for the first time since we'd met, I actually thought, "He looks handsome." His shaggy, dirty blond hair fell just right, and the faint five o'clock shadow gave him a rugged edge I hadn't noticed before. He greeted me with an easy smile and a warm hug, then opened the car door like a gentleman. As I slid into the seat, nerves flickered through me. We'd spent plenty of time together these past few months, but tonight, something felt different.

It was Saturday, and the night pulsed with life. A live acoustic band played softly from the stage inside, their music drifting out onto the patio where Daniel and I sat by a glowing gas fire pit. We shared a bottle of red wine and a few appetizers, sinking into a conversation that wove easily between his world and parts of mine.

I learned that Daniel was the oldest of four and the only boy, yet he spoke of his sisters as if they were his closest friends. So were his parents, who had never missed a game or school event. Hearing about them made me think of my dad and all the ways he had shown up for me over the years. Daniel told me about his baseball days in high school and then a year in college, until an injury cut things short. His sisters were athletes, too. His family lived just outside the city, close enough that he still saw them regularly.

The night stretched on with laughter, stories, and the comfort of good food and wine. The air was chilly, but the fire's warmth and something sparking in my heart made it feel perfect. At one point, I even shared a little about my loss. Not everything, but enough. Daniel met my words with steady eyes full of care, and in that moment, I realized I was beginning to fall for him.

When the evening wound down, he drove me home. At the entrance to my building, he leaned in and kissed my cheek. His lips were soft, and for a second, I wanted more, but I let the sweetness of that simple kiss mark our first date. Inside, I collapsed onto my couch with a smile that wouldn't fade. I texted Jackie that the night had been wonderful. She sent back a single heart emoji, and somehow, that felt just right.

As we approached Thanksgiving, Daniel and I had been dating for a month. We saw each other almost daily, and if we couldn't see each other, we at least talked on the phone. Is it possible to fall in love in one month? I had never been in love, but this felt like it had been described.

At work, Katie asked about Daniel all the time. She had finally given up on my ever going out dancing with her and her friends, but at work, she was my favorite coworker, and I truly considered her a friend. I had the feeling that she would be there for me if I ever needed her for any reason. James would sometimes chime in when Katie and I talked about our social lives. His life at home was becoming more exciting, too. He announced that he and his wife were having a baby, due in late April. The three of us continued to get together for coffee or lunch many times per week. There were times when the others in our group would join us. That's when I noticed that Paul was beginning to distance himself from me more and more. He never talked to me at church, either. I decided I didn't care. I was learning to be happy.

Happiness is slippery. It's more fleeting than I ever realized. It doesn't root itself in who you are, but in the circumstances you find yourself in. I understand that now. And I've also learned something else. You can feel happiness while sadness walks quietly alongside it. That was me then, still sad, yet undeniably happy.

I longed to call my dad and tell him about Daniel. I wished

I could tell my mom, too. It had been so long since I'd let myself think of her, but a girl needs her mom when she's falling in love. I even wondered what my brother might have thought. What would it feel like to have an older brother watching out for me, making sure I was safe?

Daniel's stories about his family, his sisters, his parents, and their closeness had stirred something in me. A sharp awareness of my aloneness. And yet, that night, my loneliness didn't eclipse my joy. Because, in that moment, my happiness had a name. My happiness was Daniel.

Crews

CHAPTER 4
Dark Eyes

Daniel's mom invited me to Thanksgiving at their house. I had met his family a couple of times by then. We had been dating for six weeks, but it felt much longer. Maybe those first few months as friends made the timing seem off. It seemed wrong to go to their home when I hadn't gone home to see my grandma since the funeral. She and I agreed that I would visit her the day after Thanksgiving instead.

I made an apple pie to take to Daniel's home. He picked me up that morning and we drove to his parents' house, the home where he grew up. They lived in a beautiful neighborhood, and their house was at the top of a big hill. It was a large, two-story home with a gorgeous pool in the back surrounded by trees and plants. As soon as we walked in the front door, the scent of turkey and dressing and pumpkin pie hit us in the face. His mom greeted us both with a big hug and took the apple pie from me, saying, "This looks amazing, Callie!"

Daniel's mom was a tiny woman, delicate in frame but striking in presence. Her hair was always styled to perfection, not a strand out of place, and her nails always gleamed as though she'd just stepped out of the salon. She dressed in dazzling clothes that seemed pulled straight from glossy magazine pages, always the latest trend, always impeccable. I never once saw her without makeup, her lipstick carefully chosen, her eyes framed with precision. She had a way of commanding a room without raising her voice, gliding effortlessly into the role of the perfect hostess. She said all the right things. Warm greetings, polite questions, gracious compliments, but beneath the polished exterior, there was something else.

I couldn't quite put my finger on it at first, but over time I sensed it, a faint stiffness in her smile, a pause that lasted a second too long, a glance that seemed to measure rather than welcome. It was as if her words were painted on, as carefully applied as her eyeliner, and though she never said anything unkind, I felt an undercurrent. Outwardly, she was gracious and charming, but inwardly, I suspected she didn't think I was good enough for her Daniel. Her presence left me both impressed and unsettled, like being offered a sparkling glass of champagne, only to find it tasted like vinegar.

We stepped into the family room, where Daniel's dad sat comfortably, absorbed in the pre-game football shows. He was an average man in every sense. Average height, a soft "dad bod," his hair thinning at the crown. But there was something easy about him, a warmth that didn't feel quite as rehearsed as Annette's polished pleasantries.

"Hey, kids!" he greeted, smiling as he rose to hug us both.

"Hi, Mr. Masters," I said, returning the embrace with a polite smile.

"Call me Bob," he insisted warmly.

"And I'm Annette," his wife chimed in, her voice light but purposeful, as if she wanted to set the tone right from the start.

Daniel's youngest sister, Jenna, sat curled up on the couch, cradling the family's miniature Maltese, a little white ball of fur named Sadie. She patted the cushion beside her and beckoned me over, her warm smile effortless as she introduced me to the dog. Jenna, with her chestnut-brown hair and matching soft eyes, was only twenty, home from college for the holiday, and already carried herself with a kind of easy beauty that felt both effortless and sincere. She was, without question, the prettiest in the family, and probably the nicest, too.

Before long, the other two sisters swept in. Amanda, twenty-seven and newly married, was all smiles as her husband, Jason, offered me a firm handshake and a polite introduction. I had met Amanda once before when she came to visit Daniel, and even then, she had struck me as a younger reflection of her mother, polished, well-meaning, but carrying that same subtle air of performance.

Leslie, at twenty-five, was the opposite. At least, that was my impression at the time. She paused in the doorway, distant, her expression unreadable, as though my presence didn't warrant much effort. I had told myself then that she was simply unfriendly, maybe even rude. But looking back now, I realize there was more to her silence than I understood at the time.

Before long, more family members arrived, including Daniel's grandparents on his mom's side, an uncle and aunt (his mom's sister and her husband), and three cousins, all in their teens and all boys. There were two big tables set up, one in the formal dining room and one in the den. Annette had the home decorated with luxurious and expensive decor in every room, and this included gold pumpkins and cornucopias. There were large vases filled with fresh flowers. There were gold candlesticks and ornate decorations throughout. My dad and I never decorated for Thanksgiving, and honestly, after my mom died, we would usually just invite my grandma over and have a simple feast for three. In the afternoon, we would watch some football, and at night, my dad and I would eat pumpkin pie and sip on eggnog while decorating our Christmas tree. I missed him, and I could feel knots in my throat. I swallowed hard to try not to cry.

Daniel and I found ourselves in the den with the cousins and Jenna while the rest of the family filled the formal dining room. His cousins, three big boys ranging in age from fourteen to seventeen, were all football players, and they could eat a lot of food. The room buzzed with their endless chatter, the kind that bounced from one topic to another without pause, like a ball tossed in a never-ending game. I sat quietly, my fork moving absently across my plate. No one seemed to notice my silence, not even Daniel.

Jenna, the tiniest at the table, somehow commanded the room whenever she spoke. It wasn't loudness or dominance that drew attention to her. It was the way she radiated something authentic, something unpolished yet magnetic.

Her kindness wasn't forced. Her laughter wasn't calculated. She didn't seem to crave their attention, and maybe that's why everyone gave it so freely. I found myself liking her more with each passing moment.

Later, after dinner had been cleared and hours of football had droned on in the background, everyone drifted outside to the pool for pie and wine. I declined both, too full to force even one more bite, and claimed a quiet lounge chair by the water's edge. The night air was cool, laced with the faint scent of chlorine, and the chatter around me blurred into a low hum. No one noticed me there, tucked into the shadowed corner of their world.

I leaned back and tilted my head toward the sky. It was black and blank, the city's glow stealing every star. How different it was from home, where the stars blazed like silver promises across the dark. I thought of my dad then, how we would lie on the ranch's old quilt beneath that endless country sky, counting constellations and whispering to the ones we loved who had gone before. We always imagined my mom and Simon among them, bright, steady, untouchable. Now my dad was with them, too.

I closed my eyes and let the ache settle in my chest. Tomorrow, I would see my grandma. Tomorrow, I could wrap my arms around her frail shoulders and breathe in the scent of her lavender lotion. The thought alone was a thread of comfort, pulling me gently through the noise of the night.

Time slowly went by, and finally, Daniel walked over to me and asked if I was ready to leave. "Yes," I replied, feeling exhausted from all the noise of the day. He asked if I was upset, and I told him that I was fine. Then we began the many goodbye hugs with his huge family before we walked out to his car to head back to my apartment.

The drive back was fairly quiet. I wasn't quiet because I was angry. I was tired and I was sad. But Daniel did not understand. He was quiet mostly, but every few minutes, he would ask, "Are you sure you're not mad about something?" I assured him that I was just tired. I did not tell him about my sorrow, about missing my dad, or about missing the stars in the sky. We arrived, and he walked me to my door and kissed me goodbye. I loved his warm, sweet kisses. They were soft and tasted like honey, a stark contrast to his rugged five o'clock shadow and shaggy hair. I had come to long for those warm embraces from him, and tonight was especially needed and left me feeling light and momentarily happy.

The next morning, I set out early for Grandma's house. The city still slept as I slipped onto the quiet roads, and soon the skyline gave way to wide stretches of open land. The drive was peaceful, almost sacred, like the world had paused just long enough for me to find my breath again.

When I stepped through her front door, Grandma burst into tears before a single word was spoken. We clung to each other for what felt like an hour, the kind of hug that makes time irrelevant. Her familiar lavender scent wrapped around me, a fragment of home I hadn't realized I'd missed so much.

We settled onto the couch, coffee steaming in our mugs, a plate of cookies between us. We laughed over old stories, cried over the losses that still ached in the quiet corners of our hearts, and flipped through photo albums whose edges had softened with time. In that moment, I thought, I never want to leave here again.

I saw the grief in her eyes, the kind that had settled there long before my father's death, the kind only a mother could carry. I remembered how she had stood beside him through the losses of my mom and Simon, steady as an oak while his world fell apart. She had been a rock for him and for me, too. But then, to lose your own child. That was a pounding, deep grief impossible to comprehend.

I wished I could be that rock for her. But the truth pressed in. I was just as cracked and worn. Neither of us needed a hero. We only needed each other to sit in the shared quiet of understanding. That was enough.

I stayed just one night. The following day slipped by with easy small talk and a quick shopping trip for groceries and odds and ends she didn't need but bought anyway. At lunch, Grandma mentioned the young cowboy who had bought the ranch. Her eyes softened as she spoke about him. A good man, she said, one who cared for the land and the animals as if they were his own.

"Would you like to drive out and meet him?" she asked gently.

I shook my head. Not yet. The thought of another man tending my dad's fields, walking his pastures, felt too raw. I was grateful he treated the place well and that Grandma liked him, but the ranch wasn't ready for me. Or maybe I wasn't ready for it. Some things need time to heal before they can be faced.

I left Grandma's late that afternoon, the sun already slanting low and golden as I merged back onto the highway toward the big city. Traffic thickened the closer I got, brake lights flickering red ahead. As the skyline rose in the distance, the sky darkened, clouds gathering like a warning. The wind picked up, rattling the bare trees that lined the road. A storm was rolling in, swift and sharp, the kind that makes the air taste metallic.

By the time I reached the city limits, the temperature had dropped, a sudden bite in the wind that made me shiver. All I wanted was to get home, wrap myself in a heavy blanket, and disappear into the familiar comfort of *Gilmore Girls*, letting that cozy, perfect little town on the screen drown out the noise of my real one.

The storm caught me just as I pulled into my garage. Rain turned to a relentless clatter of hail, pinging against the window like thrown pebbles. The wind howled down the street, shaking the trees and moaning through the cracks of my building. Within minutes, the lights went out. My apartment was plunged into darkness, the kind that feels too heavy for city living.

I lit a few candles, their flames shivering in the draft, and found a book to keep me company. For the first time in as long as I could remember, I felt the kind of fear that belongs to childhood, the unease of being alone in the dark with a storm raging outside.

Daniel texted to check on me. He was still at his parents' house, but he said he'd stop by on his way home. I wasn't sure I wanted company, but I wasn't sure I wanted the silence either. By 9:30, I was ready to crawl into bed and let the storm pass without me. Instead, I sat waiting, listening to the rain ease to a steady drumbeat and the wind's howl soften to a low hum. When Daniel finally arrived after ten, I let him in. We sat together on the couch, the soft glow of the restored lights making the apartment feel less haunted.

He held me for a while, his arms familiar but strangely distant, and kissed my cheek. He didn't ask about my trip home, about Grandma, about how it felt to step into that world again. Instead, he launched into stories about his parents' house, the decorations, the laughter, the food, all the easy, warm pieces of his life that felt so separate from mine. As I listened, I caught myself thinking, "Maybe I should decorate this place for Christmas. Maybe a little bit of sparkly magic would help."

The clock crept toward 11:30, and my eyelids grew too heavy to fight. I whispered to Daniel that I needed sleep, and we exchanged our goodnights sealed with one of those honey kisses, a balm that seemed to promise me peace as I drifted into dreams. But as he reached the door, he paused. Turning back, he murmured, "I wish you could have been with me today to decorate for Christmas." His mouth curved into a smile, yet his eyes betrayed him. Brown eyes that should have been warm flickered with something darker, something I couldn't name but instantly felt. In that moment, the honey soured. A shadow pressed against my heart, replacing sweetness with unease. Still, exhaustion wrapped me tight. It had been a long day, and sleep demanded me. I told myself not to dwell on those dark eyes. Not tonight.

Crews

CHAPTER 5
Money

My inheritance was not something I discussed with people. It was not that I was trying to keep secrets, but it was part of my life that belonged to me, my history, my father's final gift, and no one else's business. Money, I'd learned, had a way of changing how people looked at you, how they treated you, how they measured your worth. And I wasn't ready to be measured that way. If things with Daniel ever turned into something more serious, if words like engagement or marriage began to drift between us, then maybe I'd open that door. But until then, it remained closed, locked tight. My friends knew my dad had died. That was all they needed to know.

Looking back, what strikes me now is not the silence I kept, but the silence they offered in return. None of them ever asked how I was doing. Not really. I met that little group of five only days after my dad's funeral, and still, it was as though my grief existed behind a curtain they were unwilling to pull back. Maybe they thought I wanted it that way. Maybe they were too uncomfortable to try.

Except Todd. Todd was different. He didn't hover, didn't pry, didn't turn my sadness into a spectacle. But every now and then, during a late-night video game, or while the others were distracted by their own conversations, he would ask. Just a quiet, "How are you holding up?" Those few words, small as they were, felt like a lifeline. I would always give him the same answer. "I'm fine." A single, flimsy word. Fine. My shield, my disguise, my way of saying, Don't worry, I won't burden you with the truth.

In many ways, I guess it's the best word to describe me at that time. Yes, I felt the constant gnawing sorrow of loss, but I also had been given a new life and a new family. I was successful in my job, and I got along with my coworkers. Katie and I were becoming true friends. We went shopping during lunch breaks. We dragged James with us to coffee or lunch and made him tell us all about his wife's pregnancy. Her name was Pam, and although I had only met her a couple of times, I felt like I knew her so well. James truly loved her. I told myself that I wanted a marriage like theirs, one that included having a husband protect me even when I didn't think I needed protection.

When our team got together for meetings, Paul was cordial, but more and more, I sensed that he did not approve of my relationship with Daniel. I chose to believe that he was jealous because from the first day we met, it had seemed like Paul had a bit of a crush on me. As long as we got along enough to work together without drama, that was good enough for me.

The first time I realized my wealth and its significance was a Saturday afternoon of shopping with Jackie and Stephanie. Jackie was a physical therapist, and she made a great salary. She drove a nice car and wore the most fashionable outfits. Stephanie was an elementary school teacher, and she was very open about her "mountain" of college debt. She did not always complain about it, but when she did, it was awkward for Jackie and me.

We had planned a day of shopping because we were attending a holiday event with our church Bible study group. It was a semi-formal party at our leaders' home. We had agreed to meet for lunch, and then spend the rest of the day shopping before meeting up with Todd and Daniel that night to go bowling. Jackie and I delightfully tried on many dresses. Stephanie started out in a good mood, but soon became agitated. Finally, she stormed out of the dressing room area and sat on a bench, frowning.

"What's wrong?" I asked, confused. That's when the storm hit. Stephanie launched into a thirty-minute rant, her voice shaking in distress. She raged about how Jackie and I were prancing through the shops without a care, accused us of flaunting our supposed wealth, and came close to declaring us the villains in her financial tragedy.

I just stood there, stunned. *Me? Flaunting my wealth?* My car was humble, my wardrobe was plain, and my lifestyle, other than my supposed "luxury" apartment, was modest. How was I flaunting anything?

I sat on the bench apologizing for something I didn't think I was guilty of. "I am just so very sorry," I said, hugging Stephanie, "I did not mean to show off at all. I was just having fun trying on dresses and didn't realize I was bragging in any way!" Stephanie accepted my hug and my apology. Jackie, on the other hand, refused to budge. She stood beside us like an unwavering rock, unwilling to fake an apology she didn't mean.

"Steph, I love you, but you do not have the right to be mad at us because of your financial situation," Jackie said, "We did not cause this. If you are struggling to afford a new dress, you could have declined the invitation to go shopping today."

Jackie wasn't wrong, but honestly, she didn't have to drop that truth bomb right then and there. Stephanie didn't need a lecture. She needed a stage for her grand pity party. Sometimes, people just want to wallow a little. So, instead of handing her a cold, hard dose of reality, I figured a warm, apologetic hug was the better option.

Looking back on that day now, it's like someone turned the lights on in a messy room. I can see every little crack in our friend group that had been sneaking in, one awkward moment at a time. My gracious apology and what was about to come out of my mouth did not smooth things over either. Without meaning to, I seasoned a simmering pot of drama stew.

"Would it be ok with you if I bought you a dress?" I put out this question from a place of genuine care and concern. Right there on that bench, it felt kind and acceptable. If I had been on the outside, watching this like a movie, I might have noticed the turning of the tide. I might have seen the foreshadowing, the clouds and winds picking up in a storm that was stirring. My money was going to become a major problem ultimately, and not just for Stephanie.

No one spoke for a few seconds after my offer. So, I added, "I mean, I just want you to have a new dress for the party, and I have some extra money this month, and I know you would do the same for me."

Jackie shot me a look of disappointment. Stephanie calmed herself down, looked into my eyes, and, without a trace of anger or theatrics this time, said, "I don't need a new dress." I was too young and naive to truly grasp the way money weaves its invisible threads through the fabric of our lives, how it can hold people together with a fragile kind of glue, or just as easily tear them apart at the seams. I had never tasted the bitterness of debt, never felt the heavy shadow of bills stacking up like storm clouds on the horizon. To me, money was simply there, an afterthought, a convenience, not a weapon or a wedge. So when I offered help, I thought I was being generous, a good friend. I thought my gesture would lift someone's burden, not press down on their pride. I didn't understand that in the quiet world of financial struggle, an offer of help can sometimes feel like a spotlight, exposing insecurities and stripping away dignity. I thought I was giving. Stephanie felt I was taking something she could not name but deeply valued, her independence.

We left the store, Jackie and I carrying our shopping bags and Stephanie with empty arms and a blank face. Later that night, our little friend group of five was together at the bowling alley. By then, Stephanie's mood had improved a little, but there was a bit of tension. Jackie was good at ignoring it. I kept trying to make things happy. Todd bought everyone burgers and fries. He had no idea what we girls had experienced that day, but sometimes Todd just liked to do things like that. He was not rich, but he was good with money. He was working in information technology at a big downtown company. He had no college debt, and he lived frugally, so extra spending money was always available. And, Todd had a big, generous heart, so his buying us all dinner was not unusual and caused no waves.

The shopping incident was never discussed again. We moved on as if we had all signed an unspoken peace treaty. We went to the holiday event. Stephanie had clearly done a little solo shopping at some point because she arrived at the party wearing a stunning new red dress. Her curves were on display, and her red hair was styled to perfection. Jackie walked in wearing a black strapless cocktail dress, her brown hair in an updo. She looked like a supermodel, and when she walked into the room, we all stared. Daniel and I had arrived just before Jackie. I felt pretty that night. I was wearing a black cocktail dress with a big green bow. Daniel was the handsomest I'd ever seen, wearing a black jacket and a green tie. He had stopped shaving, so his beard was fuller and made him seem way more masculine. Todd finally arrived while we were standing by the kitchen bar, sipping champagne. True to form, he wore a red bow tie with a white shirt and green pants. I loved how Todd didn't care what anyone thought. He was who he was. And he was precious.

The party was a blast, one of those nights that just sparkles in your memory. Our hosts were our Bible study leaders, a polished couple in their early fifties with two college-age daughters. They ran a thriving landscaping business that had blossomed into something huge, and with it came wealth.

But not the flashy, look-at-me kind. Their home, perched high with a sweeping view of the city, whispered sophistication rather than shouted it.

And, wow, they could throw a party. The food was decadent, the games had us laughing until our sides ached, and by the end of the night, I felt like I'd been wrapped up in a warm glow of good company and great memories.

When Daniel dropped me off that night, the world seemed to pause just for us. Before I even reached for the door, his lips found mine. Warm, sweet honey melting across my tongue. One kiss became two, then three, until the air between us was thick with desire. His fingers threaded gently through my hair. My hands cupped his face as if I could memorize every line of it. Each kiss deepened, sending a shiver that rippled down my spine and bloomed in every inch of me. I wasn't just drawn to him. I was unraveling, falling hard and fast. And from the way he held me closer, I knew he felt it too.

I finally had the strength to get out of the car. He walked me to the door, and we said our goodnights with one more long-lasting embrace and one more small kiss from those sweet, yet rugged lips. I walked into my apartment, weakened by my love. I sprawled out on my bed, closed my eyes, and imagined Daniel there with me. I imagined us married, spending the rest of the night loving each other, holding each other, being one.

I was teetering on the edge of sleep when my phone buzzed. Our group chat lit up. A photo from Jackie. There we were, the five of us, huddled together by the Christmas tree, wrapped in twinkling lights and a festive glow. Our smiles were wide, our arms tangled around each other, and for a moment, we looked like something out of a holiday postcard. All the money drama, the awkwardness, the whispered resentments, none of it mattered in that frozen frame. In that moment, I had everything. A family I chose, a heart that was tumbling headfirst for Daniel, and a sliver of peace I hadn't felt in months.

CHAPTER 6
Crash

There are moments etched in my mind that can never be forgotten. I was a tiny sixth grader when my life changed forever. It was a crisp, cold January afternoon. A blanket of snow covered the school parking lot. I was wrapped up in my favorite pink coat and scarf with my purple beanie on my head. I stood there with my friends Jessica and Tracie. We had stayed late at school to finish a project for the student council. Jessica's mom was picking us up, but she was running late because of the weather. It was becoming very cold and dark as a big winter storm was approaching.

The three of us shivered as we stood in the harsh wind. There was a brief feeling of woe that hit my chest, one I could not explain. But it passed. Soon, Jessica's mom pulled up, and we jumped into her large minivan, where the heat was blasting and bags of snacks were waiting for us. Her mom never failed to bring snacks. Today's treat was white chocolate-covered popcorn. Tracie's house was the closest, so she dropped her off, and we squealed our goodbyes and began to drive to my house. I lived the farthest away on the outskirts of town, where my family owned a 1,000-acre ranch. We had cattle and chickens, and two horses named Kennedy and Joseph.

On days like this one, I loved coming home because my mom always had the fireplace lit and homemade stew and biscuits waiting for me. Winter had become my favorite season. It smelled fresh and clean, and the perfect white snow made our ranch sparkle.

I was tired and hungry and couldn't wait to walk into the front door and get a big hug from Mom before dinner. My mom always smelled like vanilla. She was the most beautiful person I knew. Her long, flowing dark hair and deep hazel eyes were radiant. My dad always said that no woman on earth had ever been prettier than his wife. He adored her. They had met in high school. They were the couple you dream of being. He played football and she danced on the drill team. They fell in love in their sophomore year, and when my dad ended up going to college several states away, they decided to get married and live in married student housing. My mom enrolled at the same school to work on her degree in education, while my dad got his degree in agricultural business.

My dad was striking in his youth, nearly six feet tall, his broad shoulders and strong frame a sharp contrast to my mom's petite five-foot-two stature. There was a quiet strength about him, a certain stillness that made his protective nature all the more reassuring. He carried himself with reserve, a man of few words but steady presence. My mom, on the other hand, was his perfect opposite. Lively, radiant, always ready to fill a room with her energy. She had that effortless charm, the kind that made her the spark of light at the center of every gathering.

When they graduated from college, they returned to their hometown, and my dad bought their first twenty acres, adjacent to my grandparents' forty-acre property. My dad was very good with money and had started saving to buy his land at the age of fifteen when he got his first part-time job at the feed store. My parents quickly settled into their new life. While they built their first tiny home on their property, they rented a small house in town. Within a year, they had finished building their first home. It was small, but over the next few years, as their funds increased, they would add onto it. Soon, they were able to purchase more land and add another 2,500 square feet to the home. They also built a large porch that wrapped almost all the way around the house. It was my favorite place on the planet.

At the age of twenty-eight, they had their first child, my brother Simon. He looked just like my dad, but he had my mom's personality. He was friendly to everyone he met. He was the most popular boy in school, but he never behaved arrogantly. I was born three years after Simon. Everyone said I looked like the perfect combination of my mom and my dad, but I had my dad's personality. I was a bit of an introvert from day one. I loved animals more than people. I longed to grow up and get married to a man like my dad, someone who owned a ranch, a cowboy who stood tall and protective.

Growing up with animals and working hard on the ranch

was the perfect life for me. In the summers, we would work so hard that we would come back to the house dripping in sweat. My mom would come out on the porch with a pitcher of cold lemonade. Sometimes we would sit out on that porch for hours and even eat dinner there so we could watch the sunset and see the stars come out. More than anything else, I loved sitting on that porch when the stars were out. They sparkled like diamonds above us.

If you had asked me then, at the age of twelve, to share my greatest desire, it would have simply been to live the life I was living. I loved my family, and I loved my animals, and I wanted that life to never end.

But it did end. It ended on that day, in that moment when I walked into my home hoping to hug my mom and sit down to biscuits and stew. Instead, my dad's cousin Shelly was there. Her eyes were red like fire, tears streaming down her cheeks. Shelly grabbed me and had me sit on the couch and spoke words I couldn't believe I was hearing. Today, I can't even remember the exact words. It felt like a bomb went off in my head when she told me that my mom and brother were dead. They had died not long before, probably while I stood freezing at the school parking lot. Apparently, it had been an instant slaughter. From what she could gather, my mom had picked up Simon at his taekwondo class. On the drive home, a tractor tire lay abandoned in the middle of the road. My mom swerved to avoid it, but her SUV caught a patch of ice and slammed into a tree. The airbags deployed, but it was of no use. They were both gone. Crushed. My dad was there now, having been whisked away by the sheriff. He had asked Shelly to come over to wait for me.

I remember sitting on the couch, numb and hollow, the world sounding distant and unreal. I think I spoke. I must have because I heard my own voice asking her to take me to them. I can't recall if I cried. Everything was a blur, a slow, spinning fog that swallowed up the hours.

I can't remember what happened next. I can't recall my father's face, or how the funeral was planned, or the people who came. What I do remember is the church, crowded to the doors, with people standing shoulder to shoulder, some waiting outside in the bitter cold. The caskets were closed after our family had one final moment alone. I wore a simple black dress. I said goodbye to Simon first. They had made him look untouched, as though sleep had simply claimed him. No trace of the violence remained. I leaned over, my voice trembling as I whispered, "I will miss you." Then I pressed a kiss to his cool cheek.

Next came my mom. The funeral home had restored her beauty with careful hands. Her hair was smoothed to perfection, her face serene beneath the soft lights. She wore her blue suit, the one that always made her hazel eyes shine brighter. How I wished they were open, just once more, to pierce through me with their familiar warmth. "Mama," I whispered, a tear slipping down my cheek, "I love you. I will always love you."

My dad and I crashed. Not in Mom's SUV that day, but in every other way that mattered. That winter, already dark and cold, grew darker, colder, bitter enough to bite. A twelve-year-old girl and her grieving father learned to cling to one another for warmth, to hold fast against a world that had lost its color.

As the years passed, they still visited me sometimes in dreams. In those early days, Mom and Simon appeared often, slipping easily into the fabric of my nights. Waking was the hardest part, the moment when memory hit like a second impact, and I would crash all over again. But time has a way of softening the sharpest edges. The sting dulled, though it never disappeared. The emptiness lingered, quiet but constant, two empty places in my heart that would never truly close. The dreams grew rarer, more fleeting, until photographs and videos became the only versions of them I had left. I held on to what I could. My mother's jewelry, her hope chest passed down from her grandmother, and my brother's high school letter jacket. Small relics of lives once lived in a bright and beautiful world.

After the accident, my mom's family, including her parents and siblings, began to visit less and less. Grief has a way of completely destroying people, and soon it claimed my grandparents, too. Their hearts were too heavy to keep carrying the weight of living, and within two years of losing Mom and Simon, they were both dead, only six months apart. My aunt and uncle, my mom's siblings, eventually moved away. Our love for each other remained, but the rawness between us was like a wound we couldn't stop touching. It made every conversation burn, every gathering feel fragile, and over time, the distance between us became more than just miles.

Crash. We all crashed. My dad tried his best to build something good out of the wreckage. He smiled when it was hard. He laughed when it didn't come easily. He became both mom and dad to me. Sometimes he even became my big brother. He was there for everything. The games, the recitals, the honor society ceremonies. He doted on me with a kind of quiet devotion that felt like armor against the emptiness.

Many nights, we sat together on that beloved front porch, the stars scattered above us like watchful eyes. We'd lean back, gaze upward, and tell ourselves that Mom and Simon were among them, shining down, keeping us company in their own glittering way.

The only comfort I found in my new life was knowing that Dad was finally free. Free from the weight of pain and the torment of grief. He was with her now, the woman he had loved most, and with the son who had made him so proud. I imagined him as a star, bright, steady, brilliant in the night sky.

But I was a city girl now, and the stars had vanished behind the haze of buildings and neon lights. Maybe that was what I needed, to not look up, to not be reminded of what I'd lost. I told myself I was grateful for this new life, and in many ways, I was. But sometimes I wondered if all this noise and light was only camouflage. Perhaps, without realizing it, I was bracing for another crash.

Crews

CHAPTER 7
Christmas

The first Christmas after losing my mom and brother felt like stepping into a world forever changed. My dad, grandma, and I escaped to the mountains, seeking solace in a small cabin tucked beside a frozen lake. The days unfolded quietly, our footsteps crunching along snowy trails, the sharp winter air biting our cheeks. Evenings were spent with warm cookies melting in our hands as the fire crackled, voices low as we sang carols that moved between sorrow and hope. We shared stories, clinging to our memories through laughter and tears. That year, we chose not to wrap gifts in bright paper or tie them with ribbon. Instead, we wrapped our grief in generosity, sending what we would have spent to my mom's favorite charity, a foundation that grants underprivileged children the gift of education. In that act, it felt as though a piece of her love lived on, glowing quietly in the dark of winter.

After that Christmas, Dad and I were determined to keep

the holiday spirit alive at the ranch. We made it our tradition to decorate on Thanksgiving night. Then we would sip eggnog in the twinkling lights.

Now I was learning what Christmas in the city is like. To my surprise, I found it enchanting. The city always glittered after dark, but during the holidays, it transformed into a galaxy of color. Strings of lights draped from rooftops and lampposts, shop windows glowed like jeweled treasures, and every street seemed alive with a special kind of magic. I even began sleeping with my blinds open, letting the colors spill into my room at night. Reds, greens, golds, and blues, like little bursts of starlight, keeping me company until morning.

My friends and I had planned a gift exchange and pizza party at my apartment. Daniel and I had already made it festive, our tree standing proud, dressed in lights and ornaments we had placed together. On the day of the party, Jackie came early, filling the kitchen with laughter as we cooked side by side. We layered lasagna, brushed butter over garlic bread, and pulled brownies from the oven, their tops dusted with peppermint sprinkles like tiny sparkles of winter magic. I kept catching myself pausing in quiet disbelief. How had I landed here, in this cocoon of warmth with a boyfriend I adored, a best friend at my side, and a circle of people who poured love into me as if I had always belonged to them? So much had changed, so suddenly. A move to the city. A grief that nearly broke me. And now this, my sparkling, full, and lovely life.

That night, the five of us played board games and laughed. We filled our bellies with good food and our hearts with joy. A few times that evening, I noticed that Stephanie and Todd were more flirty than usual. The thought of them potentially becoming a couple was delightful. She, with her spunky honesty, and he with his giving heart, would make such a sweet match. I kind of began picturing them going on double dates with Daniel and me when it hit me that the fifth wheel in the group would be Jackie. Dear Jackie! I really wished I could find her the right guy to date. She was so pretty and smart. Surely we could find someone worthy of her.

Before long, it was approaching 2:00 in the morning. I have never been a night owl, and I couldn't believe we'd been eating and playing all that time. Jackie was the first to say, "Well, everyone, a girl's gotta get her beauty sleep at some point." We all hugged goodbye. Jackie, Stephanie, and Todd walked out the door.

Daniel stood by the wide living room window, the city lights reflecting in his gaze like distant stars. When he turned toward me, something in the glow of his eyes called me forward, pulling me as if by an invisible thread. My steps trembled with anticipation until I reached him, and then, suddenly, I was lifted into his arms. He held me with a strength that felt unshakable, his right hand tracing slow, tender circles across the small of my back. Shivers of desire rippled through me. With his left hand, he brushed along the curve of my neck, sliding upward to my jaw, then to my cheek, tilting my face toward his. His lips found mine in a kiss that deepened with exquisite slowness, parting my lips open, his tongue sweeping against mine in a dance both gentle and electric. My whole body tingled, alive from head to toe, as though every nerve sang. His caresses grew more urgent, his kisses more consuming, and I felt myself dissolving, spinning helplessly into a weakness I did not want to resist. In that moment, all I wanted was him. His kiss, his arms, his love, forever.

Time slipped away until we were lost in each other, our bodies pressed close, the air between us thick with heat and longing. But then, I turned my head, gently lifting his hands from me. My voice was barely a whisper. "You better go."

He understood. We both did.

Years ago, I had promised myself that the only man who would ever intimately know me would be my husband. Daniel, though no longer a virgin, carried his own vow. After his past, he had resolved that he would not give himself to another woman until marriage. In a world where intimacy had become casual, even expected, we chose differently. We chose to honor our faith, to honor the people we would one day marry, and to honor the meaningful, beautiful possibility of "us."

So we stopped. Breathless, trembling, but resolute. We brushed off the dust, rose from the floor, and walked together to the door. There, with the weight of unspoken desire hovering between us, we exchanged a goodnight and a goodbye.

As Christmas Eve drew near, Daniel's family invited me to join their holiday celebrations. The pressure was there, gentle, unspoken, but heavy all the same. I told Daniel I couldn't, that my grandma would be alone, and I needed to spend the holiday with her. More than that, I wanted him to meet her, to visit my home, and see where I came from, but he did not seem at all interested.

Looking back, I realize how blinded I was by the haze of

romance. If I hadn't been so swept up in the rush of love, perhaps I would have recognized the first threads of control tightening around me. His family was everywhere, woven into nearly every corner of his life. Sunday dinners, endless holiday gatherings, impromptu game nights that seemed mandatory rather than optional. And Daniel, at twenty-nine, spoke with his mom almost every single day. I wondered if that was normal. But in my heart, unease had already begun to stir.

Daniel and I had our first fight. I stood my ground about Christmas with Grandma. There was no bending, no compromise in me. What stung even more was his resistance, his unwillingness to step into my world, to see the place and people who had shaped me. He wanted me woven seamlessly into his life, yet he refused to enter mine. His words cut sharp. He accused me of being rude to his family, reminding me of how many dinners, how many gatherings they had opened to me. Then, as if it were the final blow, he said I should be grateful. Grateful to have such a "wonderful" family extending their love to me. Grateful? The word echoed inside me like a slap. My blood rushed hot with disbelief. I was being asked to trade my own roots, my own people, for a place in his carefully guarded world, and I was expected to thank him for it.

In the end, I caved. I told my grandma that I would visit her the day after Christmas. Daniel told me he might go with me. He would decide at the last minute because one of his cousins had tickets to a football game and all the guys in the family wanted to go together. "It's our bonding time," he smiled. Daniel certainly had a lot of bonding time with his family.

We arrived at Daniel's family home on the morning of Christmas Eve. We spent that day cooking and baking and watching holiday movies. Everyone from Thanksgiving was there again. I hardly talked to anyone. Jenna was the only one who seemed to notice I was there. Well, Sadie the dog did too. Daniel spent most of his time playing video games with his cousins. Annette and her sister, along with Amanda and Leslie, gossiped in the kitchen. I mostly sat on the couch wishing I were anywhere else.

We all got dressed up for a candlelight Christmas Eve service at their church. When we walked into the building, it was obvious that the Masters family was popular. There were many greetings, many hugs, and then many photos. I had noticed that their home was filled with framed family photos all throughout the house. And here we were taking more. We posed in front of the big Christmas tree in the lobby and then in front of the large window overlooking the courtyard with all its lights. There were photos of just the girls, then just the guys, then just the cousins, and then couples. Daniel and I posed for ours in front of a group of poinsettias.

The church service was lovely. We sang carols in candlelight. We heard a message of Jesus' love. We bundled up in our coats to leave, and as we approached the door, I heard a woman's voice squeal, "Danny!"

Daniel's hand slipped out of mine as the young woman approached us. He grabbed her in his big arms and joyfully hugged her. "Kendall, I've missed you," he shouted. Then Annette and Leslie ran over to hug Kendall, too. They certainly seemed to like this girl. Through overhearing bits of their conversation, I understood that Kendall was a family friend, that her parents were good friends with Annette and Bob, and they all went way back.

Although it felt like an eternity, Kendall was probably only with them for ten minutes. Still, in those ten minutes, I stood quietly to the side, invisible, as Daniel, his mom, and his sister shared many stories and then their goodbyes with her. Their laughter rose and fell easily, like a melody I wasn't part of. One by one, the rest of the family drifted outside until soon they were all gathered together on the front steps, voices overlapping, faces glowing with joy.

Meanwhile, I remained inside, exactly where Daniel had left me. For a moment, a sharp thought flickered through me, "Would they even notice if I wasn't there? Would they pile into their cars, still laughing, still talking, completely unaware that I had never followed along?" The answer stung, but I knew myself too well. I wasn't going to play the girl who pouted in silence, waiting to be sought out. So I smoothed the feeling from my face, lifted my chin, and slipped toward the door. Stepping into the chilly evening air, I quietly folded myself into the middle of their big, buzzing group, careful not to disrupt the current of conversation. Together, we all made our way to the parking lot, their voices filling the night as I walked alongside them.

I slept in one of the guest rooms that night, tucked beneath crisp sheets in a house that wasn't mine. I don't cry often, but alone in that room, the weight of it all pressed down until the tears came. They soaked my pillow as I lay there, staring into the darkness. This was my first Christmas as a true orphan. The word itself felt heavy, foreign, something I had not yet let myself realize until that moment.

Around me, the house was filled with family, Daniel's family laughing somewhere down the hall, voices carrying through vents and walls. Yet even surrounded by their noise, I felt like a ghost. I wanted to scream into the quiet, to claw at the anguish in my chest. More than anything, I wanted to pick up the phone and call my dad, just to hear his voice, just to know I wasn't entirely alone. But phones don't reach heaven. So instead, I buried my face into the pillow and let the sobs come. In that moment, I wasn't part of the big family. I was just a girl without parents, curled up in a strange room on Christmas Eve, aching for what I had lost. Of all my Christmases, this one carved the deepest wound. This one left me empty, tormented, and lonelier than I had ever been. And for the first time since my dad's funeral, I cried myself to sleep.

Christmas morning arrived in a rush of voices and footsteps. One by one, cars pulled into the driveway, and soon the house was overflowing with grandparents, uncles, aunts, and cousins. I lost track of how many. The big family room became a sea of flannel and cotton because, to my amazement, everyone showed up in pajamas. Yes, even those who had driven over that morning arrived in their sleepwear.

The night before, we had each opened a single gift, matching pajamas. Everyone had them, right down to Sadie the dog, who pranced proudly in her tiny plaid set, tail wagging like she knew she was part of the tradition. To my surprise, there had been a package for me too. I had slipped mine on reluctantly at first, but as I made my way down the staircase that morning, the laughter and the sight of so many smiling faces in the same silly outfit softened me a bit. In the family room, someone had already set up a camera on a tripod, angled perfectly toward the tree. We gathered around, jockeying for space, tugging at pajama sleeves, pulling kids to the front. For a moment, I stood there, feeling like an outsider peeking in, but then Daniel pulled me over, and just like that, I was swept into the fold. With matching pajamas and holiday chaos swirling around me, I found myself smiling (at least on the outside) as the timer blinked red. Together, we posed in front of the glittering tree for a large family photo.

I endured Christmas at the Masters' home, moving through the day as though I were playing a part in someone else's holiday story. At one point, I slipped away and called my grandma. We talked for a while, and I was relieved to know she wasn't spending the day alone. She was with my dad's brother and his family. Still, I couldn't shake the feeling that I should have been there with her, not here. My presence in this big house felt unnecessary, almost invisible. If I had vanished, I doubted anyone would have noticed, including Daniel. He spent most of the day wrapped up in games and laughter with his cousins and sisters, their closeness a reminder of what I didn't have.

Gift opening came in a flurry of torn wrapping paper and cheerful exclamations. Annette, in her flawless way, handed out box after box, showering everyone with expensive things. Love, for her, seemed to flow most naturally in the form of material abundance. I was included in her generosity. Along with the matching pajamas, she had piled gifts into my lap. A plush blanket, a basket of spa items, a sleek name-brand travel bag, and a silver picture frame holding a photo of Daniel and me. It was as though she was trying to script me into their story, to place me firmly within the family portrait.

Late that night, Daniel drove me back to my apartment. Unlike most drop-offs, this time, I did not long for that honey kiss. This time, I was mentally and emotionally worn out. He sensed my exhaustion, so he did not press the idea of staying with me for a while. He wished me a safe journey on my travel home to see Grandma the next day. He had decided that he could not join me this time because he had a "busy work week coming up" and "needed some rest after a busy holiday." Daniel worked as a paralegal at a law firm. There were some big trials coming up in the new year, and he had a lot of research to do. I told him I understood. But did I really?

Was it truly fair that I was expected to be there for every Masters family gathering, every outing, every little tradition he shared with them, yet he never once showed the slightest interest in meeting my grandma or seeing my hometown? I couldn't help but wonder if my world, my roots, meant nothing to him at all. If the people and places that shaped me were so easily dismissed, what did that say about how he saw me? Was I anything more than an accessory, someone to drape on his arm and parade around for the sake of appearances, while the essence of who I was went unseen, untouched, unvalued?

My visit with Grandma was a balm to my soul. Her warm embrace, the shared ache of our losses, and the gentle hush of her little home stitched something back together in me. We dined on a leftover casserole my aunt had made, then wrapped ourselves in the glow of a patio heater as a soft snow drifted down around us, coffee cups warming our hands.

We talked about Dad, about Mom and Simon, about neighbors and friends, and all the good people of our small town. Grandma told me the mayor planned to put up a plaque in Dad's honor come January. He had left a mark there. He and Mom both had. They were raised in that town, rooted in it, and they had given generously to charities, to neighbors, to anyone in need. Mayor Jackson wanted the town square to remember that. I promised Grandma I would come back for the unveiling.

As I pulled away from Grandma's little apartment and drove toward the highway, a dull ache bloomed in my chest. I didn't want to leave. Why had I chosen a life so far from here? Why had I ever believed that a bustling city could fill what was empty in me? I needed Grandma. I needed my town. I needed my little ranch.

Tears blurred the road as the memories rushed in. Nights on the porch, stars sparkling above. I told myself I'd done the right thing by selling it. Hadn't I? But that morning, leaving hurt more than I could have imagined. "Don't cry, Callie," I whispered, tightening my grip on the wheel. Then I pressed the gas, merged onto the highway, and drove myself back to the city.

Crews

CHAPTER 8
A New Year

On New Year's Eve, Daniel and I attended a wedding. One of his college friends had thrown a celebration that shimmered with cheer and champagne. We danced until our feet throbbed, spinning under strings of lights as the music carried us past midnight. The hurt I'd nursed from Christmas seemed to melt away that night. His distance over the holidays had stung, but somewhere between the music and the glow of the room, my longing for him stirred again. And when the clock struck twelve, his kiss ignited a rush of warmth that spilled straight into my heart.

I was in love. And that night, after our goodnight kiss melted away any uncertainty, I finally let the words escape. "I love you," I whispered, smiling up into his dark, steady eyes. I didn't care whether he said them back. I just needed them out in the world before they burned a hole inside me.

"I love you too," he breathed, not to my face, but against my left ear. The warmth of his breath, the softness of those words, sent a shiver racing down my spine. We stood there in the doorway, wrapped around each other, swaying as if the night still played its music. Now, the only song playing was the beating of our hearts.

And with that, the race began. Once those three words were spoken, everything seemed to accelerate. Jackie took it as her cue to start planning our wedding, our future, our forever. I wanted her to slow down. We weren't engaged. We were in love, yes, but that was all. Jackie, however, was convinced that by year's end we'd be married and well on our way to a bright, charmed life together.

Soon enough, the whole friend group knew. Daniel and I had become the "it couple" at church, the pair everyone seemed to expect would last. They noticed the way our fingers intertwined as we strolled through the foyer, as though even the walls themselves paused to watch us pass. They smiled at the quiet intimacy we shared, the way his arm curved naturally around me while the steam of our coffee rose between us. In the parks, older couples would pause in their steps, their eyes soft with memory, and say things like, "You two are just so darling. You remind us of ourselves when we were young, and everything felt like forever."

I floated on those moments, on their words, their knowing smiles, as if they were small blessings scattered along our path. I felt beautiful, not just in the way I looked, but in the way being beside Daniel made me glow. Standing with him, I felt part of something vaster than my own small world, something warm and steady and full of promise. This, I thought, was what love was meant to be. A soft constellation of glances, touches, and quiet affirmations that told me I belonged.

My only irritation was how much time we were spending at his family's home. We spent many Sundays there for dinner. His father was always gracious, greeting me with a hug and a polite question about work, to which I'd give my usual, noncommittal "fine," and then slip into the background as Annette, Bob, and Daniel carried on their conversations about people and things I didn't know. It was Sadie who kept me company. She had no reservations, no expectations, just a warm little body in my lap, licking my face until I laughed. As it had always been in my life, animals offered the truest kind of welcome, and I simply liked them better than people.

As mid-January approached, Daniel agreed to head to my hometown for the unveiling of my dad's plaque. Grandma was excited to meet Daniel, and I felt like this would be the beginning of a true commitment. I picked him up early that Saturday morning, and our drive home was pleasant. It was bitterly cold, but inside the car was the warm glow of love and happy conversations.

Grandma welcomed us with her familiar, enveloping hugs, the kind that made everything feel a little more right. I drove us to the town square, where people were already beginning to gather. Proudly, I introduced Daniel to the people who had watched me grow up. The townsfolk greeted him with genuine warmth. They asked about his family, his work, his hobbies, leaning in, truly listening, as if eager to welcome him into their circle. They treated him the way I had wished his family would treat me, with open curiosity and the simple kindness of wanting to know him.

Dad's plaque was beautiful. It was mounted to a sign

outside the courthouse that read, "In loving memory of Michael J. Williams, whose generosity will continue to flow through town." Simple and kind, just like Dad. Grandma shed a tear. I held her hand. Daniel put his arm around my waist. I hugged everyone there and departed.

We ate an early dinner at a cafe my grandma loved, then we left town. I did not want to go. I felt myself longing to stay in the town so familiar, so sweet, so "home." It seemed like every time I returned, the desire to never leave swept over me.

I dropped Daniel off at his place shortly after 10:00. I did not get out of the car. Before he opened his door, he leaned over to kiss me. He swept his finger across my forehead and tucked my hair behind my ear, then said, "I love you."

"I love you too," I replied. Then I drove back to my apartment feeling the fullness of love, but the emptiness of loss, feelings I would learn would walk with me many times over my life.

The winter was icy cold. It did not snow much, but the streets were often very icy, causing my boss to have us work from home more than usual. That made the days feel lonely. I missed the many coffee and lunch dates with Katie and James. We shared several funny jokes and memes on our Microsoft Teams meetings. James told us that Pam was officially in her third and final trimester and that she was getting much bigger. He loved feeling the baby kick, and he told us the exciting news that he was having a boy. Katie and I, along with our boss, Betty, began to plan a baby shower with a basketball theme. James didn't play basketball, but he was a huge fan, and he couldn't wait to take his son to games.

February was extremely cold all month long. With the winds and ice, it was often too difficult to get out and do anything, but my friend group made sure to get together for dinner and game nights often. More and more, it seemed that Stephanie and Todd were growing closer. They refused to confess their feelings, but we could all see their relationship growing. Daniel and I grew closer, too. We saw each other every day. Jackie seemed both happy for us and also sad about herself. She was lonely. There didn't seem to be anyone for her to date. Stephanie and I suggested that she try a dating app, but Jackie did not feel comfortable meeting someone on an app. She wanted what she called "the old-fashioned way of meeting someone."

Her birthday was at the end of the month. None of us was sure how to handle it. On the one hand, we wanted to celebrate our friend, but on the other, she was not excited about turning twenty-eight. For her, it seemed like she was too close to thirty now, and that was her "scary age." But in the end, we decided to throw a small party. We decorated my apartment in purple, her favorite color. We had a big cake, pizza, and lots of gifts. Jackie had a great time. Toward the end of the party, while she and Daniel sat on the couch, I walked in from my bedroom, where I was grabbing a sweater. I noticed Daniel looking at her. She was shuffling a deck of cards, staring down at them. His eyes were on her, and for a brief moment, I felt uncomfortable. Jackie was a beautiful woman. Her olive complexion and deep dark eyes, and thick hair, along with her height, made her look like a movie star. We all thought she was a picture of perfection, but seeing Daniel look at her that night sent a punch of envy my way. When we all first met, I had thought that Jackie had a crush on Daniel, but when the two of us began dating, she was so happy about it that I quickly stopped believing it.

It wasn't long before I forgot about that incident. My focus was on my budding romance. I continued to crave those honey-sweet kisses and long conversations. I threw myself into our relationship. I gave him my all. Daniel did not ask me about my family. I told him about them anyway. I told him how crushed I was to lose my mom and brother. I told him about the grief I was still enduring over the loss of my dad. He listened when I talked, but I began to notice that he never really tried to engage with me or comfort me. It was like he thought I should just move on. I told myself that he just didn't understand because he had never lost anyone he loved. His whole family was alive and just down the road.

And they were a constant in our lives. Sunday dinners soon became Sunday mornings at church, too, which meant some very long Sundays. And sometimes, there were Wednesday dinners. I would get home from work to have Daniel waiting there to take me to his parents' house. We would eat, hang out in the family room, where they would talk again about things unrelated to me. I would spend my time petting Sadie and get home late, exhausted.

I never complained openly about the vast time spent with Daniel's family, but he confronted me one night. "Why do you always act so stand-offish?" he asked.

Stunned, I told him I didn't understand. I had never seen Daniel so annoyed. He explained that he'd spent the day before shopping with his mother, and that's when the truth began to surface. Looking back, that moment should have been my first yellow flag, the signal that I was wading into dangerous waters. Annette had told him outright that she didn't think I was a good match for her son, that I didn't involve myself enough in their family's world. Worse still, she said that Amanda and Leslie agreed with her, convinced their brother was heading down a path of regret.

Silence thundered between us, heavy and unrelenting. I sat beside Daniel, stunned, as the minutes dragged by, each one stretching longer than the last. The quiet pressed in until I wanted nothing more than to disappear into it. At last, I found my voice. "I don't even know how to respond to all of that," I said softly. Then, after a deep breath, I asked the question that burned the most: "Do you feel the same way about me as your mom and sisters?"

"I don't know what I think right now, Callie," he replied. He looked down for a moment, then back into my now watery eyes, his own dark eyes pushing deep into my soul. At last, he spoke in a softer tone, yet still alarming. "I just wish you would be more open and friendly to my family and try to fit in."

At my core, I've always been an introvert. I know how to set aside my quiet nature, how to smile and be talkative when the moment calls for it, but beneath it all, I am a calm, country girl who treasures silence, who finds her peace in animals and open skies. Daniel's family was nothing like me. It felt as if he wanted me to mold myself into their image, to shed the essence of who I was just to fit in. And if that was what he needed, did he truly love me? Or did he only love the version of me he hoped I might become?

When a new year begins, most people think of resolutions, a chance to start fresh, to do better, to chase down goals. Was Daniel asking me for something far greater? Was he asking me to resolve to become an entirely different person? The thought terrified me. Was this what I was supposed to do? How I wished my dad were here. He would know what to say. He always did.

CHAPTER 9
Flags

I've never been much of a beach lover. I didn't grow up anywhere near the ocean, but in high school, I spent two weeks each summer at my friend Tracie's family beach house. While Tracie and her siblings chased waves on their surfboards, I preferred slow, wandering walks along the shore, my eyes scanning for shells. I never cared much for the salty water clinging to my skin, but I loved the rhythm of the waves crashing and the chorus of seagulls overhead.

It was there that I first learned the language of the flags. Green flags mean everything is steady and sure, safe waters, clear skies, no storms on the horizon. They signal that all is as it should be, that the current is gentle, the path inviting. Yellow flags mean moderate hazard, in which the surf and currents are strong enough to keep you cautious. Red flags mean high hazard when the water turns dangerous. Then there were the rare double red flags, the ones that closed the ocean entirely, forbidding anyone to enter.

People often talk about flags in relationships, but I had never truly been in a committed one, so when Stephanie asked if I had noticed any, I didn't know how to answer at first. Still, my thoughts went immediately to Daniel's family, not just the way they treated me, but how deeply entangled he seemed with them. Was this simply a close-knit family, or something tipping toward control? Was his bond with his mother a normal son's devotion, or was she pulling the strings? If he catered to her every whim, what would that mean for a future wife? Would she always come second? It felt like a yellow flag, a warning of potential hazards ahead. But was it shifting, quietly, into red?

By March, the bitter cold began to loosen its grip. The wind still swept through the city with a sharp edge, but every so often, the sun would break through, spilling warmth across the courtyard of my apartment complex. On those rare, golden afternoons, I would claim a weathered bench, a book in one hand and a cup of tea in the other, letting the soft light settle over me. It wasn't the tranquil hush of my ranch, but it offered a brief reprieve from the city's relentless hum, a quiet pocket where my soul could catch its breath.

Work had become extremely busy, pulling me in deeper each week. My long hours stretched even later. Seven o'clock became my normal quitting time, and by the time I stumbled through my apartment door, exhaustion wrapped around me like a heavy blanket. All I wanted was sleep.

Daniel was far from understanding. He complained often that I wasn't giving him enough of my time, and insisted I show up at his parents' Wednesday dinners even if it meant arriving near eight. On those nights, his frustration was clear.

I was "making his family eat late," as if my job were a personal inconvenience to them. I felt torn, stretched thin between the demands of my work and the demands of a man who claimed to love me.

Then, unexpectedly, Paul and I shared our first real conversation in months. It started innocently. He needed clarification on some numbers in a spreadsheet, but soon the topic drifted elsewhere. To Daniel. I had always sensed disapproval in Paul's silence, a quiet judgment he never quite voiced. But this time, it felt different. There was something almost protective in his tone, like that of an older brother watching me walk a thin edge. He didn't criticize Daniel outright, yet his words held an undercurrent, subtle but steady, hinting that the flags I felt might not be all in my head.

One breezy, cool Friday evening, I came closer than ever to ending it. Daniel's words had been a steady drizzle at first, criticism after criticism. I didn't spend enough time with him or his family. My quietness was somehow rude to his mom and sisters. I didn't smile enough, didn't talk enough, didn't anything enough. For nearly an hour, I sat there, letting each word chip away at the fragile peace I tried to carry.

And then came the sentence that cut straight through me, sharp and cold as a blade:

"You act like your grief, like your sad little life, is worse than anyone else's problems, and that's pretty selfish."

The world went still after that. Even the breeze outside seemed to pause.

In that moment, the flags went from yellow to red. Had I

been wise, I would have screamed at myself to get out. "Get out of the waters, Callie! You are going to drown!"

At twenty-two, I don't think I was experienced enough to know what to do. Another "not enough" to add to the growing list he'd been crafting for me. Somehow, I managed to leave that night with my pride destroyed, but my chin high enough above the waters so that I did not sink. I did not get my normal dripping with honey kiss goodbye. Instead, I got a quick hug and an "I'll call you tomorrow after we have both calmed down." But I had been calm. He was the raging storm.

At first, I was determined to swallow my emotions. I would not talk to Jackie and Stephanie about how Daniel was making me feel. I realized that I didn't really share much with either of them. Then I wondered, "Who do I share with?" Was I such an introvert that I never opened up and shared with the people in my life? Was I always like this? Was Daniel right about me? Was I closed off and rude?

Thus began my slow, spiraling descent into self-loathing. I convinced myself I was unworthy, a terrible human being, someone who had somehow failed at life before it had even properly begun. I searched back through the two decades of my existence, combing through memories like pages in a book, desperate to find proof that there had ever been anything good in me. The strange thing was, no one at home had ever made me feel that way.

I had friends growing up, not the wide circle Simon always seemed to gather around himself, but sufficient for me. My best friend was Tracie. We met in kindergarten, two quiet girls who found each other the way kindred spirits always do.

She wasn't as introverted as I was, but she wasn't the kind to crave the spotlight either. Somewhere in the middle, she was my balance.

While the other kids raced across the playground, shrieking with laughter and climbing the monkey bars, Tracie and I would wander to the far edge of the schoolyard, where the trees grew close together and the ground smelled of earth and grass. That was our secret kingdom. We hunted butterflies and ladybugs, collecting tiny treasures in our cupped hands, marveling at the beauty in small, overlooked places. Out there, among the leaves and sunlight, I felt seen, understood, safe.

Maybe I should have stopped immediately and called Tracie. Or Grandma. Or anyone from home because all I could feel at that moment was insecurity. Next came the doubts about my decision to move to the city. At first, they whispered at the edges of my mind, but soon they grew louder, heavier, until they became impossible to ignore. And with them arrived the most troubling thought of all, the one that cut the deepest. Did my move to the city kill my dad?

The question gnawed at me, circling endlessly. If I had stayed, would things have been different? Would he have felt less alone, less burdened by the silence of the house? Would his heart, already fragile, already broken, have found just enough reason to keep going if I had been there with him? I couldn't stop myself from imagining him in his final moments, wondering if my absence had widened the emptiness around him. Maybe he had finally let go because I wasn't there. Maybe he died of a broken heart, and maybe I was the one who broke it.

Pain gripped me, leaving me motionless in my apartment while thunder cracked and lightning tore open the night sky outside my window. The storm felt like a reflection of what was raging inside me. Loud, violent, unrelenting. My phone sat on the table beside me, glowing in the dark, but I couldn't bring myself to reach for it.

I thought of Jackie and Stephanie, but something in me hesitated. It didn't feel right to call them. Todd crossed my mind, too, but I quickly dismissed the thought. What would I even say to him? And Daniel. I imagined his voice, not gentle or comforting, but reprimanding, telling me to toughen up and stop feeling sorry for myself. So I sat there, alone, torn apart by the questions spinning through my mind.

These people were supposed to be my people, my family of choice. Shouldn't I want to call them when I hurt? Shouldn't they be the ones I could lean on without fear or shame? But instead of comfort, I felt judged. Were the red flags only about Daniel, or was there something deeper, something broken in the fabric of my friendships, too? The thought chilled me more than the storm ever could. It was as if I were caught in a rip tide, pulled farther and farther from shore. I could see the waves towering above me, feel the undertow dragging me down, and I wondered if I was already too far out, thrashing in waters too treacherous to escape. Was I about to drown, not from the storm outside, but from the storm within?

Somehow, I managed to wipe away the flood of tears and reach for my phone. I didn't even know who I was going to call. My hand just moved, as if something deep inside me knew I couldn't stay alone in that storm of thoughts. Katie's voice burst through the line, bright and bubbling, "Hey, Chica!" In an instant, her squeal of joy and her carefree tone cracked through the heaviness. I felt myself exhale, almost smiling.

It was Saturday, and I was supposed to meet up with my friend group later, but the very thought of being around them made my chest tighten. They felt like the last people on earth I wanted to see. So instead, I asked Katie what she was doing. Without missing a beat, she flipped the question back to me, then invited me to go dancing with her and her friends.

"Yes," I said, surprising even myself. That was it. A single word, and I had made a decision. I would pull myself together. I would go out dancing. I sent a quick text to my friend group, "Not feeling well, can't make it tonight." Yes, it was a lie. No, I didn't care. I didn't even bother reaching out to Daniel separately. One message to the group was enough.

Then came the transformation. I slipped into a sparkly outfit that shimmered in the light, the kind of thing that felt like armor and celebration all at once. I brushed on makeup, painted on a smile to match, and styled my blonde hair until it bounced with intention. Fancy heels buckled at my ankles, clicking with promise against the floor.

When Katie finally pulled up, I ran down the stairs, my heart pounding with something that felt dangerously close to excitement. I hopped into her car, leaving behind the heaviness of the evening, ready to trade it all for music, dancing, and a night of freedom. I wasn't going to sit in the dark, drowning in doubt. I was going to dance my cares away. All the flags were green, and the waters were clean, clear, and fresh. I would swim through them with pure joy.

CHAPTER 10
Control

I grew up on a picturesque 1,000-acre cattle ranch just outside a charming little town filled with honest, hard-working people. It was a rare gem in the modern world, a place where life moved more slowly, where kindness and generosity weren't exceptions but expectations. At the time, I didn't see how rare it was. It was all I had ever known, what many would call the simple life.

I watched enough movies and television to understand that most people didn't live the way I did, but it wasn't until I moved to the city that I fully grasped just how pure and special my upbringing had been. Even my college years felt simple in comparison. I attended a small university, just forty-five minutes from home, nestled in another quaint town, with barely 5,000 students.

During my freshman year, I lived on campus with a roommate named Jennifer, a lively and funny eighteen-year-old from a large farm about six hours away. She was studying agricultural business, just as my dad had years earlier, with dreams of returning home to take over the family farm alongside her two younger brothers. Her family was close, the kind of close that felt natural and warm, not the suffocating closeness I would later come to know in Daniel's family.

Those college years were a season of slow, steady revival. The anguish of losing Mom and Simon was a constant, but little by little, I began to breathe more deeply again, to feel sunlight where there had once been so much gray. I made many new friends, most of them from small towns, farms, or ranches, just like me. The college had a strong reputation for its agricultural business program, though I chose accounting, a field that suited both my gift for numbers and my quiet enjoyment of them.

Jennifer and I threw ourselves into everything that made campus life vibrant. We played co-ed intramural softball, joined a cozy Monday night Bible study in our dorm, and spent countless late nights in a little coffee shop that stayed open until one in the morning, cramming for exams and laughing until our stomachs hurt.

Most weekends, I drove home to spend time with Dad. But on the weekends I stayed behind, I wandered the serene ponds and sprawling parks scattered across campus, often with a book in hand or simply letting the stillness settle into me. I worked hard, yes, but I played hard too. And for the first time in years, life felt full and gently bright again. My friends weren't consumed by appearances or cliques. They were easy, kind, and fun, and I soaked in every bit of it.

Jennifer met Kyle about two weeks into our freshman year,

and from the start, they seemed to circle each other like two stars destined to share the same sky. Over the next few years, their connection deepened until love between them became undeniable. By the close of our sophomore year, in those last weeks before summer break, they announced their engagement.

By then, Jennifer and I had moved off campus into a small apartment with two other girls, Christy and Lisa. Life felt full but comfortable. When Jennifer married Kyle, they settled into an apartment just a few blocks away, and Christy, Lisa, and I welcomed a new roommate, Hayleigh. I got along with all of them easily. I was still the quiet one, but somewhere between shared dinners, late-night talks, and the hum of daily life, I found myself opening up more than I ever had before. Not spilling my deepest scars, but sharing enough that I felt, at last, like I belonged, and like I was slowly, quietly, coming alive.

I graduated a year ahead of schedule, thanks to summer courses. At twenty-one, with my degree in hand, I stood at a crossroads. Dad and Grandma quietly hoped I would return home, back to the familiar comfort of our land, but something in me stirred, an urge to taste the unknown, to test myself against the pulse of city life.

It was, in many ways, unlike me, the quiet, country girl who found comfort in the hush of open fields and the steady company of animals. Yet, there was a pull, subtle and persistent, whispering of streets I'd never walked and nights where the air buzzed with a different kind of life.

I interviewed on campus with a large firm in the city, and when the offer came, I said yes. Telling Dad was the hardest part. I saw the flash of worry in his eyes, the one he never could quite hide when it came to my safety. Cities were too loud, too fast, too full of unknowns. But he didn't try to stop me. That wasn't his way. He loved me enough to let me go, to let me grow. He even helped me find my first apartment. He inspected every detail. The gated entrance, the fob-secured doors, the ever-present security team. It wasn't the ranch, and it wasn't quiet, but it was close to work and, in his own cautious way, he approved. Proud of me, even. He never stopped telling me he was proud. He was a great dad.

Most of my friends still had another year left in school, but they filled the stands that day, cheering as I walked across the stage to receive my diploma. The sun was warm on my shoulders, the air buzzing with applause and the rustle of gowns as graduates lined up one after another. When my name was called, I felt the surreal mix of nerves and pride that comes with both an end and a beginning.

Afterward, I was surrounded by hugs, handshakes, and promises. "Keep in touch, don't be a stranger, let's get together soon." Their words wrapped around me like a soft blanket, bittersweet and fleeting. I knew life was already pushing us in different directions, but in that moment, it felt possible that we could hold onto the threads of friendship.

Driving away from campus later, the familiar buildings shrinking in my rearview mirror, I let gratitude wash over me. This place had blessed me with good friends and peace for three years. I left that day with a sense of hope that the future waiting for me held promise.

But now, there I was, questioning everything. Every choice I had made, every step that had seemed so sure at the time, now felt shaky beneath me. On paper, my life looked whole. I had friends, I had a boyfriend, and I had a good job. Things people my age were still chasing. Yet inside, I felt as though all the pieces that should have made me complete were only loosely held together, threatening to scatter.

Just months earlier, in the raw aftermath of my dad's death, I had clung to those very things. My new friends who had become like family, the rush of falling in love, the structure of meaningful work. They had been lifelines, carrying me through the darkness and even giving me moments of real happiness. But now, the happiness seemed to slip through my fingers.

What was happening to me? Was it all unraveling at once? The friendships, the love, the fragile sense of belonging I thought I had built? Or was it me, breaking apart from the inside, unable to hold onto the joy I had found?

I started piecing together the reasons behind my sudden insecurity, thinking I might make sense of the unraveling. Of course, there was the night Daniel let loose, his words sharp, his criticism relentless, cutting into me in ways I hadn't expected. That wound still stung, but it wasn't just him. What struck me even more was the realization that when I'd been hurting most, I hadn't reached for my closest friends. I hadn't felt safe enough to call Jackie or Stephanie or Todd. Instead, I dialed Katie, a coworker, because somehow her easy, bubbly energy felt more like relief than the people I was supposed to call my family.

That night, my phone buzzed with text messages I didn't read, calls from Daniel I deliberately ignored. For once, I let them go unanswered. Instead, I threw myself into the music, the swirl of lights and movement on the dance floor. It wasn't the best night of my life, not even close. But it was what I needed. Enough to let the hurt inside me loosen for a few hours, enough to quiet the questions and numb the pain. For one night, I let myself forget.

The next morning, I scrolled through the barrage of messages. I typed out a quick text to Jackie: "Sorry about last night. I still don't feel great so I'll be skipping church this morning." Short, safe, impersonal.

The group thread had spiraled from mild concern into full-blown interrogation. At first, it was, "Hope you're okay, Callie!" and "Check in when you can." But as the hours passed without a response, their tone shifted, worry sharpening into impatience. "You need to let us know what's going on!" one of them demanded, as if my silence was a crime.

Daniel's messages hit hardest. A few texts, then two voicemails. His words weren't tender or patient. They were sharp, demanding. "What is your problem, Callie? You need to call me and let me know what's going on. Are you really sick, or are you just sulking about last night?" His voice felt like a shove instead of a hand to hold. I stared at my phone, dreading the thought of calling him back. So, I crafted a careful, neutral text, something that wouldn't reveal the storm inside me. "I don't feel well. I need rest. Skipping church."

What happened next was a great silence. And somehow, that silence bruised more deeply than the two-hour lecture criticizing me ever could. No texts. No calls. By Sunday night, the absence of his voice felt like a punishment, heavy and deliberate, pressing down on me until I could hardly breathe.

Finally, my phone lit up. It was Jackie. She wasn't calling to comfort me, though. "What's going on, Callie?" she asked, her tone cautious, careful. "I mean, I'm starting to think you're not really sick. It just seems like maybe you didn't want to be with us."

I hesitated, then let the truth spill. I told her about Friday night, how Daniel had torn into me, how he accused me of being unfriendly, how his mom had labeled me cold and rude. I thought, foolishly, that Jackie would hear the rawness in my voice, that she'd rush to defend me, to reassure me that I wasn't the villain in this story. I thought she'd say she was sorry and that Daniel and his mother were out of line.

But instead, there was a pause, and then, softly, she said, "Do you think maybe you could try to be a little more outgoing with his family? A little more engaging?" Her words landed like a stone in my chest. It wasn't advice I heard. It was an agreement, confirmation of the very criticism that had already been eating me alive. I wanted compassion. I wanted understanding. I wanted her to say no one should have to change who they are to be accepted. And I thought she, of all people, would get it, because Jackie isn't flashy or high-energy either. She's calm, measured, sometimes quiet. Surely she'd understand. But instead, it felt like she had stepped to the other side, joining Daniel and his mom, leaving me stranded on my own little island, branded as cold, rude, unworthy.

Monday morning was busy at work, and I was grateful for the distraction. It kept my mind from circling back to

Daniel's silence, to Jackie's words. Katie showed James the photos from our night out. She was so proud, so delighted that I'd finally joined her world. I smiled at the pictures and slipped into character. I told her I'd had the best time, that I couldn't wait to go again. But inside, I knew the truth. The dancing hadn't been magic. It had just been a lifeboat at a time when I was drowning.

Monday night arrived, and with it, nothing from Daniel. Is this what ghosting feels like? Todd and Stephanie had checked in, wondering if I was feeling better. I decided to send simple texts back to let them know I was better and thanked them for checking on me. But I was determined to wait for my emotions to calm before reaching out to Daniel.

I scrolled through the photos on my phone, each one a painful punch to my gut. There we were, his arm draped around me on a wedding dance floor, my cheek pressed to his shoulder. We looked every bit the couple in love, wrapped in that dizzy, sparkling illusion. Another swipe, another memory, us surrounded by friends near a glowing Christmas tree, our smiles wide, our eyes bright as if joy were effortless, endless. We looked like the happiest people in the world.

But looking at those frozen moments now, I felt the emptiness behind them. When did it shift? How did something that appeared so full slip so quietly into the abyss? What fragile thread had snapped when I wasn't looking?

And then, suddenly, a text. Daniel. "Can we talk?"

I didn't text him back. Instead, I called. He answered with a voice soft as silk, almost tender. "Hey, Cal," he said, as though the storm from Friday had never passed between us.

We talked for two hours. Two full hours on the phone, something I'd never done in my life. The conversation wandered back to that painful Friday night, yet no apology ever left his lips. What he offered instead was space for me to speak, and I did. I told him how deeply my heart had been bruised. But somehow, by the end of it, the tables had turned. It was my voice carrying the apologies.

I apologized for not being the woman he wanted, the one he thought he needed. I promised I'd try harder. I even said I was sorry for missing Saturday night and Sunday morning, as if my absence had been some great betrayal. How did I let myself get pulled into that spiral so easily? Daniel's sweetness was like syrup, so thick, so sticky. It left me feeling as though I owed him. And now, here I was, ready to mold my soul into something foreign, just for the promise of being loved by him and his family.

But, is that love? Or is that surrender?

Looking back now, I can see it clearly. The sharp sword of control, sliding quietly between my ribs and piercing my heart. At the time, I was too young, too tender, too eager to belong. Grief had already carved its spaces within me, and into that emptiness I was willing to pour anything that resembled love, even if it was only the illusion of it. I was desperate, whether I admitted it or not, to have a family, to somehow replace the one that had been snatched from me.

Daniel, I would soon learn, was tethered by invisible strings to his mother. And now, without even realizing it, I was being pulled by his. The control didn't arrive with flashing lights or warning bells. It crept in quietly, disguised as care, wrapped in words that felt like love. I didn't see it happening. It unfolded right under my nose, and before I knew it, I was already entangled.

CHAPTER 11
Road Trip

Toward the end of March, our friend group planned a long weekend getaway. We rented a charming lake house, loaded Todd's SUV with luggage and enough food to feed an army, and hit the road. Four hours of winding country roads stretched before us, dotted with budding trees and the coming of spring. We stopped at a roadside fruit and nut stand, smiling as we sampled the delicious treats.

The drive was alive with energy, stories flowed, songs spilled from the speakers, and joyful noises filled every mile. I sat in the back, Daniel on my right and Jackie on my left, while Todd drove with Stephanie in the passenger seat. There was a little extra sparkle in their banter, a flirtation that was becoming much more profound.

When we finally arrived, the house welcomed us with its wide wraparound deck and breathtaking view of the water. We unpacked and claimed our rooms, us girls sharing the big bedroom that overlooked the lake. Outside, spring was spreading out her charm. The trees were just beginning to bloom, and the lake shimmered as though scattered with diamonds. Everything felt so fresh and alive.

Our days were filled with sunlit adventures, hiking through rugged trails, gliding across the lake in kayaks that cut through the glassy water. Evenings found us gathered around the fire, bellies full from hearty dinners we cooked together, laughter spilling over board games scattered across the floor.

Daniel and I carved out stolen moments amidst the fun, quiet strolls by the lake, fingers laced together, whispered flirtations exchanged in the cool dusk air. We kissed beneath the budding branches, the world around us brimming with the newness of spring. His thirtieth birthday was just a week away, so we decided to throw him a surprise celebration. Jackie had snuck a homemade cake into one of the coolers. I splurged on his favorite thick, expensive steaks, while Stephanie and Todd brought along a handful of cheeky "over the hill" decorations. Cliché, yes, but charming in their way.

While the others scurried to decorate, I lured Daniel out for a stroll around the lake. When we returned, the house erupted with a chorus of "Surprise!" We grilled the steaks, feasted like royalty, and presented him with the gift we had all chipped in for, a sleek smartwatch he'd been eyeing for months. His face lit up, a mix of pride and boyish delight as he basked in the attention. He hugged everyone, then kissed me softly, leaning in to whisper his thanks.

Sometime in the night, long after the house had gone still, I stirred awake. The clock glowed just past two in the morning. Faint voices drifted in from the family room, low, hushed, too deliberate to be the innocent rustlings of a late-night snack.

We had all said our goodnights hours ago, retreating to our rooms around eleven. My first thought was Stephanie and Todd. Had their playful flirtation turned into something secretive under the cover of darkness? I glanced at Stephanie's bed. She was there, sound asleep, her breathing even. But Jackie's bed was empty.

A flicker of curiosity, and something sharper, rose in me. I slipped quietly to the door and eased it open, the floor cool beneath my feet. There, on the couch, sat Jackie and Daniel. Side by side. Too close. Their voices a low murmur, their heads bent just slightly toward one another. I couldn't hear the words, only the soft cadence of them, like a secret not meant to be shared. But I could feel the wrongness of it. The hour, the hush, the closeness. Something about the scene pressed cold fingers to my chest.

Should I step out and make my presence known? Or stay in the shadows, ears straining for any scrap of truth? My pulse thundered as the questions twisted like a blade. Was I about to witness betrayal unfold before my eyes? From the start, I had caught glimpses of Jackie's fondness for Daniel. A long glance here, a too-bright smile there. But she had been the first to cheer when he and I began dating, the loudest to celebrate when I said we were in love. Had all that been theater, carefully staged to mask her own yearning?

And Daniel. I remembered that night in my apartment, the way his gaze had paused for a fraction too long on her. Just a heartbeat, nothing more, or so I had told myself. He had never given me reason to think his feelings for her were anything but platonic. She was beautiful, yes, but I dared to believe I was the only one who held his heart. Now, in the dim hush of the night, the picture before me twisted that belief into something fragile and trembling. Were my best friend and my boyfriend really out there on that couch, weaving betrayal while I lay just steps away?

With a sudden burst of courage, I spoke. "What are you two doing up?" Stunned, they turned toward me. Jackie's face was flushed, revealing both surprise and guilt. Daniel's face showed no guilt at all. He slowly got up and walked toward me, and asked why I was awake.

"I heard noise," I murmured, stepping into the glow of the family room. Daniel rose quickly, his expression unreadable, and guided me to the couch. I sat beside Jackie, while he lowered himself onto the floor near our feet, as though this were the most natural thing in the world. But it wasn't. Not for me. Not with the air humming with something unsaid. Jackie and I felt it, the weight, the awkwardness, while Daniel seemed completely oblivious. Or was that his mask?

On the coffee table, an open bottle of wine glinted in the firelight, two half-empty glasses standing beside it. I caught Jackie watching me notice them. "I couldn't sleep," she blurted, her voice soft, rushed. "So I came out for some wine. Daniel wandered in right after, so we both poured a glass, and, well, the time just got away from us." She smiled, a quick, clumsy one, and added, "We were just talking about old friends, people from before you were around." I stayed only a few minutes, my skin prickling with discomfort.

"I'm going back to bed," I finally said.

"I'm going too," Jackie replied instantly, almost too eagerly, as if she wanted to erase the picture that had already been painted in my mind. But it was too late. Her flushed cheeks, her bumbling words, the way her eyes darted, it all sketched the reality I hadn't wanted to believe. She was utterly, unmistakably smitten with my boyfriend.

A few hours later, the sun was beaming through the window, and the scent of freshly brewed coffee beckoned me to the kitchen. I slipped on a robe and went out to see Todd in the kitchen cooking eggs. He was wearing a Star Wars apron. Everything with Todd was Star Wars or Star Trek or some geeky thing. Somehow, it made him adorable. "Want some coffee, Callie?" He asked warmly. I happily took a cup and sat on a barstool to chat with him while he finished making us all breakfast. What a thoughtful friend Todd was.

Before long, Stephanie wandered in, her fiery red hair swept into a careless bun, eyes still heavy with sleep. She padded across the kitchen in her polka-dot pajamas, offered a drowsy "morning," and wrapped her hands around a steaming mug of coffee. Sliding onto the barstool beside me, she let out a soft sigh, the kind that comes from a night too short and a bed too cozy to leave.

The three of us settled into easy conversation. Todd eventually clapped his hands together, declaring it was time to eat. "Let's not wait on Jackie and Daniel. They'll get out here when they get out here," he joked. Todd's breakfast was a feast of perfectly scrambled eggs, bacon, and toast with jam. We ate, we lingered, we started clearing plates and wiping counters. And then Jackie appeared. She drifted into the room like a ghost of herself, pale, dark circles shadowing her usually bright eyes. Jackie was the type who never seemed to try, yet always looked polished, radiant even without a trace of makeup. But that morning, something in her was dimmed. Her hair was tousled, her shoulders slumped, her natural glow replaced by a kind of quiet exhaustion.

It grew later and later in the morning. Daniel had not yet surfaced, but the rest of us were showered and packed and ready to leave. Eventually, Todd woke Daniel up and told him we had to get going. It was a long trip back to the city, and we all had to be at work the next day.

Daniel was in a bad mood that morning. He'd missed breakfast, only managing to gulp down a quick cup of coffee, and he didn't have time to shower. He shoved his belongings into his bag, and then we loaded up to leave.

The drive home carried none of the lighthearted joy of the ride there. Stephanie and Todd talked to each other in the front seats, their chatting a low hum that did not drift back to us. Jackie stared out the window. Daniel slept for most of the ride, his head tilted against the window, breath slow but heavy. When he finally woke up, his mood had softened only slightly, enough to complain about how hungry he was. Todd offered to swing through a drive-thru, but Daniel waved it off, muttering that it wasn't worth the wait. Instead, he settled for a pack of gas station donuts.

Todd pulled into our church parking lot, the same place where our adventure had begun just a few days before. One by one, we unloaded our bags, the cheerful energy from the start of the trip now a faint memory. I reached for my luggage when Daniel caught my arm. "I'm going straight home," he said, his voice flat but not unkind. "Hot shower, real food. I'll probably crash early tonight. I'll call you tomorrow sometime."

He kissed my forehead, not my lips. The smallest detail, but it made something inside me shake. I swallowed the lump in my throat, nodded, and watched as he walked away, tossing a quick, "Thanks, everyone, for the watch and the surprise party!" over his shoulder. At least he remembered to be grateful.

Todd and Stephanie waved as they climbed into their vehicles to leave. Jackie met my eyes for a brief moment as we both unlocked ours. Her wave was quick, almost nervous. I waved back, but my chest felt tight with questions I didn't dare ask. What had started as a bright, carefree road trip had twisted somewhere along the way into something brittle and strange. My heart now felt like a roller coaster of lurching highs and quiet drops. I needed to stop spinning. That night, I went home, curled up on the couch with Gilmore Girls, and let myself drift into an early sleep.

Crews

CHAPTER 12
Katie

At twenty-four, Katie carried herself with the kind of confidence and poise you'd expect from someone twice her age. Growing up near a bustling mountain resort town, the daughter of two successful attorneys and the younger sister of a medical student, she could have easily been the type to flaunt privilege. But she wasn't. Katie's intelligence was obvious, though never the kind she used to outshine others. Instead, she wrapped it in gleeful affection and a boundless enthusiasm for life.

Everything about her radiated fun. She dressed in outfits that always seemed effortlessly adorable, the kind that made you wonder how she managed to look put together even in jeans and a hoodie. She zipped around town in her Jeep, top down whenever the weather allowed, hair whipping in the wind, music blasting. Katie never met a stranger. She had a way of pulling people in, as if friendship with her was inevitable. And she was never in a bad mood. Even on gray days, she carried the sun with her. Simply put, it was impossible not to like Katie.

Her brother was in town for a medical conference just a block from our building, so Katie and I made plans to meet him for lunch. Jack was, without a doubt, Katie in male form, just as talkative, just as magnetic, brimming with energy that seemed to spill into every corner of the room. He was studying pediatric oncology, yet despite the weight of such a serious field, his presence was light and easy, like a breath of fresh air.

The three of us sat at Oskars, picking at our steak salads and laughing so loudly I half-expected the waitstaff to hush us. It felt like medicine to my tired, worn-out soul, as though the joy between siblings spilled over and healed me, too. Halfway through the meal, Jack leaned in with a grin and announced his latest news. He and his longtime girlfriend, Stacie, were engaged. Katie's squeal rang out so sharp and delighted that the entire restaurant turned to look. Instead of being embarrassed, she only laughed harder, hugging Jack across the table.

I couldn't help but watch them and wonder. If Simon were still here, would we be like Katie and Jack, vibrant, teasing, alive with stories to tell? Would I have loved the girl he chose, joining in his excitement as if it were my own? Sitting there with them, I found myself imagining Simon was sitting there with us, laughing along.

More and more, I found my bond with Katie growing stronger. From the start, I had been grateful to have a coworker I could grab lunch and coffee with, but as time marched on, she became the friend I enjoyed being with the most. I told people that Jackie was my best friend and that my little friend group from church was my "family," but if I were being more honest with myself, I would have had to admit that relationship was feeling strained, while things with Katie were easy, light, fun.

Katie radiated a kind of joy I hadn't yet understood. I had already learned how fragile and fleeting happiness could be, how easily it dissolved when life turned cruel. But Katie embodied something deeper, something rooted not in circumstances, but in choice, in hope, in quiet faith.

She carried light into dark places. Even when she spoke of her cousin's battle with childhood cancer, a story drenched in suffering and loss, she found meaning where most would only find tragedy. She remembered how their family had rallied, how neighbors and strangers formed a net of support, how a community rose to fight for a ten-year-old's fragile life. And though her cousin did not survive, Katie focused on the courage this precious child had shown and on the delightful moments they had shared in between the hospital visits.

Her optimism wasn't naive. It was resilient. It was not born of an easy life, but of a decision. To choose hope over hurt, joy over anguish. Being near her, I began to see that happiness didn't always mean everything was right. It meant believing that light was still worth reaching for, even when the night was long. That beauty could form from the ashes.

As time went on, I found myself wanting to be more like Katie. I would never be the sparkling, bubbly, outgoing person she was, but I could learn to see the color in the world again. I could close my eyes and think about Simon and smile. I could slip on my mom's jewelry and feel her presence brush against mine. I could visit my hometown more often and see my dad's plaque, reminding myself of what a good and decent man he was. And while I was there, away from the city lights, I could look up at the stars and remind myself that my family was there, twinkling above, cheering me on from a place I could not see with my eyes, just with my heart. They would welcome me home someday, when my race here on earth was done.

Yes, the weight of my grief while I remained here would never fully lift. But like Katie, I could learn to choose where to rest my gaze, not on the ache of what I'd lost, but on the beauty of what I'd had, and the promise of what was still to come.

A few days after our lunch date with Jack, Katie and I found ourselves tucked into a corner booth at our favorite coffee shop, the rich aroma of roasted beans filling the air between us. Steam rose lazily from our mugs as the early afternoon light spilled across the table, warm and golden. Somewhere between sips of coffee, the dam inside me cracked. Words began tumbling out, hesitant at first, then with a force I could no longer restrain. I told her about that night with Daniel, the one that had festered in my mind ever since, when his voice turned sharp and instructive, when he chastised me for being too "closed off" with his family as if my heart owed them entry on command. I confessed how his affection had started to feel less like love and more like a leash, tugging me into a version of myself I didn't quite recognize.

And then, almost in a whisper, I admitted the thing I'd

been swallowing for weeks. My uneasy suspicion that Jackie might harbor feelings for him, too. Each confession left me feeling exposed, raw, as if I were peeling my own layers back one by one. Katie didn't flinch. She didn't interrupt. Not once did she rush to offer advice or pass judgment. She simply held the space, her eyes steady, listening intently while I vomited out my distress.

When I finally finished unloading, spent yet strangely lighter, she reached across the table. Her fingers curled gently over mine, warm, grounding, steady. "Chica," she said softly, her voice a balm, "when we see flags, we move ourselves to safety. If you need to move to safety, I am here. You are not alone."

It was such a simple string of words, yet they landed with the weight of an anchor, pulling me back from the storm in my mind. I didn't just hear them. I absorbed them, felt them thread through the tightness in my chest, loosening something I hadn't realized I'd been clenching for so long. In that moment, I knew Katie wasn't just a friend. She was the kind of person who plants herself beside you like a shield when the wind starts to howl. The rest of the day felt different, lighter somehow. I moved through it as though someone had quietly unhooked the invisible weights from my shoulders. My steps felt longer, my breaths less shallow, and for the first time in weeks, I felt free.

Crews

CHAPTER 13
New Life

Tax season had us buried under mountains of paperwork, but amidst the clatter of deadlines, our office buzzed with a very different kind of energy, one of streamers, balloons, and exciting plans. We were in full swing, preparing a baby shower for James and his adorable wife, Pam. The office had transformed into a playful little court of celebration. Orange streamers looped from corner to corner, tiny basketballs dangled from strings like ornaments, and miniature hoops sat on desks as both decoration and game. Even the cake joined in on the theme, crowned with a giant, frosted basketball and the words piped in cheerful icing, "Welcome Baby Brady."

The air was thick with the sweetness of frosting and the sound of stifled laughter. Pam walked in, tiny as ever, her frame delicate yet carrying a belly so perfectly round it looked like she had smuggled in the very prop we'd all been decorating with. Each step she took was slow, careful, as though she were balancing a small world before it was ready to roll out into ours. She was glowing, in that way only expectant mothers seem to, like her skin caught the light differently, soft and hopeful.

I found myself watching her and thinking of what babies do to us, not just their parents, but to everyone expecting their arrival. They have this uncanny power to pull the future a little closer, to make us think of beginnings rather than endings. Seeing her there, beaming despite her awkward waddle, I felt a stirring in my chest, a quiet reminder that life keeps offering us new chances. Babies are proof of that. They whisper of clean slates, of breaths that smell like milk and morning, of seasons that come not to replace the old but to refresh the tired corners of our hearts. In that moment, between the basketballs and the streamers, hope felt tangible. It had a name, Baby Brady, and it was almost here.

In my own life, I found myself leaning toward hope, deliberately this time, as if I were choosing it from a shelf and setting it down carefully in my heart. The awkwardness between Jackie and me hadn't vanished entirely. There were still moments where a silence stretched a little too long, or a glance carried something unspoken, but the weeks since the road trip were softening, fading. Our little friend group seemed to have moved forward, stepping out of that shadow and into something lighter.

Daniel and I, to my quiet relief, were in a better flow. His sharp edges had dulled a bit. He wasn't as quick to criticize, and when he reached for my hand, it was with something warmer, more deliberate. There were still questions tucked away in the corners of my mind, but for now, I let myself breathe.

Meanwhile, Todd and Stephanie announced that they were officially a couple, not that any of us were truly shocked. The news felt more like a curtain being drawn back on a play we'd all been watching from the wings. Their relationship was endearing. Stephanie turned thirty-one in April, and we marked the occasion with dinner, flickering candles, her laugh carrying over the table. Todd, three years her junior, somehow carried himself with an old-soul steadiness. There was something sweetly protective in the way he hovered around her, brushing a strand of hair from her face or tucking an arm around her shoulders like it was second nature.

Stephanie, of course, remained the same unfiltered spark in our circle, never shy about saying exactly what flashed across her mind, often to our delight and occasionally our embarrassment. Daniel and I even joined them for a couple of double dates, the four of us carving out our own little time of fun and inside jokes. And yet, each time, a small tug of guilt popped into the back of my thoughts. For eight months, we had been a group of five. Now, with our cozy foursome clinking glasses over dinner, Jackie was conspicuously absent, and something about that emptiness felt like a chair pulled back from the table, waiting.

One bright Saturday afternoon, I invited Jackie to lunch. We chose a small café downtown with an outdoor patio that overlooked the slow-moving waterway, its surface sparkling like scattered diamonds beneath the sun. We chatted over our favorite grilled chicken salads, the tang of citrus dressing mixing with the warm scent of freshly baked bread. Around us, the world was alive. Children's laughter chimed like bells in the distance, ducks glided by in their gentle, squeaky procession, and the sky was a flawless stretch of blue without a single cloud to soften its brilliance. The sun's golden light kissed our faces, and a playful breeze swept through our hair.

Lunch felt effortless, the kind of easy, relaxed style that Jackie and I always seemed to fall into. We talked about work, about our mutual obsession with Gilmore Girls, and about the new boutique opening near her apartment. For a while, it was simple. Uncomplicated. Almost perfect.

And then, as though the universe had decided to stir the water, a young couple passed by, hands intertwined, heads bent toward each other in that quiet space lovers often share. I caught the moment Jackie saw them. Something flared across her face, a swift shadow, a tightening around her smile. The brightness of the afternoon seemed to dim, just a little. She drew a slow breath and let her guard down. The words tumbled out. How her sister's marriage was a constant reminder, how every friend seemed to be either married or well on their way, and how she felt left out. Alone. Without a shred of hope that her own story might one day unfold differently.

My heart hurt deeply for her. I couldn't fathom why love had eluded her when she had so much to give. She was graceful in the quietest ways, intelligent, and calm, kindhearted in a manner that remained long after her presence. It baffled me, and in that moment, all I wanted was to promise her something I couldn't, that the waiting would end soon. Isn't life full of seasons? And wasn't this one just beginning to turn? Somewhere deep down, I chose to believe that her Mr. Right was already on his way, close enough, perhaps, to catch the same golden sunlight we sat beneath that day. Hope. Sometimes you just have to hold onto it.

And what about my own hope? Was I hoping for something that was just as impossible for me as Jackie's was for her?

In my daydreams, I had always pictured the tender, almost cinematic moment when my future husband would sit across from my dad, hands probably damp with nerves, and ask for my hand in marriage. I imagined my dad leaning back in his chair, wearing that familiar stern expression that masked his playful heart, pretending to be intimidating, drawing out the moment just to make my guy sweat a little, while deep down bursting with pride and barely containing his joy that his little girl had found love. I always saw them as friends, those two, laughing over a steak dinner, talking about ranch work, maybe even conspiring to surprise me. I had always, always hoped for that.

But life had rewritten that chapter before it even had a chance to be created. My dad was gone, and no fantasy could stitch that reality back together. When I let myself imagine Daniel asking me to marry him, that sweet vision came tinged with a sharp pain. There would be no father to ask, no protective handshake, no knowing glance passed between the man who raised me and the man who wanted to walk beside me til death parted us.

It was then that I realized something deeper. How truly single I was. Not just unmarried, but completely untethered. I didn't even have a big brother he could go to, no father figure waiting with an approving nod. The picture I had carried in my heart for years, of my dad walking me down the aisle, the wide-open sky over our family ranch arching above us, vanished like smoke. It had never struck me so fully until that moment. If Daniel did ask, his would be the only family filling the pews on our wedding day.

Yes, I had relatives, aunts, uncles, cousins, and a grandmother. But only Grandma was truly close by, and even she lived five hours away. The thought of standing in a white dress with barely anyone on the bride's side of the church sent a strange ache twisting through me. Who would help me choose the dress? Who would steady me in that moment, whisper the kind of marriage advice only a mother can give?

The swirl of grief and longing rose high for a moment, threatening to drag me under. But I had learned something in this season of my life. I could choose what to hold on to, what to focus on. "What would Katie do?" I asked myself, and the question made me smile despite the heaviness. Katie would find the light in the room, even when the shadows felt thick. So I took a deep breath, let the ache settle quietly in its corner, and let my thoughts wander back to Daniel and the quiet certainty I felt growing between us. We had been together less than a year, but I felt it in my bones. The proposal was coming. And this time, I chose to let hope sit beside the sorrow.

Our regular dinners at his parents' house continued as always. I did my best to nod along, to smile at the familiar names of people I'd never met and places that belonged only to their shared history. It was a world with its own language, one I was still trying to translate. When Jenna visited from college, though, the air felt different. Jenna had a way of turning her attention outward. She asked questions about my work, my family, and my favorite little corners of town. Her curiosity felt like an open window in a stuffy room. Annette, on the other hand, never really ventured past the polite surface. She didn't know much about me, and from what I could tell, she didn't seem especially interested in changing that. Bob would occasionally chime in when Jenna pulled me into the conversation, but his interest felt half-hearted.

One quiet Sunday, after church, we all gathered in the dining room, Annette and Bob at either end of the table, Daniel beside me, Jenna across from him, with Amanda, Leslie, and Jason filling the remaining chairs. The scent of roasted chicken and warm bread hung in the air as hands reached for dishes and passed them down the line. The clink of silverware against porcelain was the steady background to their familiar, well-worn conversations.

Then, in the middle of passing a basket of soft dinner rolls, Jenna turned her curious eyes toward me. "Is Callie short for something," she asked, "or is that your full first name?" The table paused, just briefly. I felt the shift, the weight of every gaze, even Daniel's, settling on me. For a strange moment, a thought flickered, "Does he even know?"

"It's short for Calista," I said, offering a small smile. There was a murmur of acknowledgment, then the noise of the conversation picked up again, back to their world, their familiar threads. No one asked more. No one stayed with me. I sat still for a heartbeat longer, rolling the sound of my full name around in my mind like a stone warmed by the sun. Calista. My mother had chosen it to honor her grandmother, her Greek roots winding their way into my life through a name that meant "most beautiful," "lovely." Only my mom ever used it. To everyone else, I was just Callie or Cal when they were feeling especially casual.

That night, as Daniel kissed me softly goodbye, he whispered in my ear, "Goodnight, Calista." That familiar surge of love soared through me.

The next morning, James was absent from work, and it wasn't long before I learned why. Pam's water had broken during the night, and they were at the hospital, where she would spend nearly a full twenty-four hours in labor. I had never experienced childbirth myself, but I imagined how exhausting and overwhelming it must be, how every contraction, every breath, must stretch a person to their limits. It made me think about birth itself, how we all enter the world through such a harrowing, incomprehensible ordeal, and how merciful it is that our earliest struggles are erased from memory.

All that pain and endurance, however, culminated in something miraculous. The birth of a perfect baby boy. A tiny bundle of love and joy, wrapped in the warmth of his parents' hearts, ready to fill their lives with a new kind of awe, tenderness, and uncontainable emotion. Brady James McKinney arrived with flawless, round cheeks and soft, fuzzy hair that caught the light in a halo of innocence.

The next day, we received three precious photos. In the first, Brady was snug in a rubber ducky blanket, a tiny blue hat perched on his head, his little fists curled in contentment. In the second, James cradled him carefully in a rocking chair, pride written in every line of his face. In the third, Pam held him close in her hospital bed, her own exhaustion etched into her features, but her smile radiated pure, unguarded joy.

Seeing those images brought tears to my eyes. Here was a life untouched by sorrow, by mistakes, by heartbreak, fresh and unmarked, a symbol of hope for what the future could hold. I knew life would eventually introduce its trials and pains, but for now, Brady existed as a perfect pause, a moment of pure happiness. His very presence reminded us all that even after the most difficult, painful journeys, joy and love could bloom anew. A baby had arrived, and with him, the world seemed just a little brighter.

My world seemed brighter, too. After the uncertainty of the road trip, I had found myself questioning everything. Daniel, my friendship with Jackie, my life in the city. But in the weeks that followed, a sense of clarity began to settle over me, like sunlight breaking through clouds. Katie had been my anchor, my steady voice of wisdom and comfort, whispering words that would echo in my heart: "When we see flags, we move ourselves to safety. If you need to move to safety, I am here. You are not alone." I would remember that, but for the first time in months, it felt as though the flags were gone. Spring had arrived, carrying nothing but green flags, gentle breezes, and warm sunlight that seemed to seep into every corner of my soul.

With my happiness restored, my mind wandered freely to the life I longed for with Daniel. I imagined a life of marriage to him, the laughter spilling over morning coffee, the quiet evenings curled up in our home surrounded by mementos of our love. I pictured children playing in sunlit rooms, tiny feet pattering across hardwood floors, the smell of baking filling the air as we prepared meals together. I imagined a small plot of land not far from the city, where we could build a weekend cabin, a place for fishing, for adventures, for sunsets watched in peaceful silence, our children at our sides.

My dreams reached into the seasons yet to come. Holidays gathered around a sprawling table, voices rising in joy and gentle teasing, love threaded through every conversation, every glance. I pictured a little boy, whom I would name Simon Michael, after my dad and brother, carrying forward the legacy of those I loved most. And a little girl, Alyssa, a name to honor my mother, whose kindness and warmth I hoped to see reflected in her tiny hands and bright eyes.

I felt it all, the goosebumps along my arms, the warmth of the spring sun against my skin, the thrill of life's fresh beginnings, and I let myself smile. I allowed myself to imagine a future blooming with love, with family, with hope. My new life was budding, and for the first time, I felt ready to step into it, arms open, heart unguarded, and soul fully awake to all that was yet to come.

CHAPTER 14
My Mom

Alyssa Simon, my mom, was born into a lively, boisterous family, the kind where joyful noise bounced off the walls and every meal felt like a celebration. The Simons were a hard-working farm family on the north side of the county, the kind who rose with the sun and carried the love of the land in their bones. Mom was the second child, nestled between her spirited older sister, Tanya, and the youngest siblings who followed. Tanya, two years her senior, was what people called a tomboy, quick as a whip, climbing trees higher than the boys dared, racing across fields on her four-wheeler, and throwing a baseball with the kind of fierce accuracy that left everyone impressed.

When Mom was just a year old, little Heather arrived, bringing another swirl of energy into the household. Heather was quieter than the rest, but she could keep up with them all. She was a skilled barrel racer in the rodeo, and she loved animals like the others in the family loved people. A year after she was born, the only boy in the family came along. My Uncle Jacob grew tall and handsome, with a mischievous charm that made him irresistible to his older sisters. He was also thoroughly spoiled, a dynamic that continued into his adult years, though tempered by the loving structure of his wife, Aunt Erica.

As a child, I adored spending time with Mom's family. Their home was full of warmth, easy laughter, and stories that seemed to stretch forever. My grandparents, Anna and Dale, shared a long friendship with my dad's parents, Ruth and Jeb, and the two families celebrated together whenever a milestone came along. Their joy had been palpable when Mom and Dad married, and it only intensified with the arrival of my brother, Simon. Even as a toddler, Simon possessed a magnetic charisma. He charmed everyone he met, and Mom's family couldn't resist showering him with affection, much like they had done with Uncle Jacob. But Mom and Dad were determined to keep him grounded. They guided Simon gently yet firmly, teaching him that charm without character was vain, and that his goal should always be to grow into a faithful, loyal gentleman. Watching them raise him, I could see the balance of love and discipline, and how it shaped the teenager he became, someone whose warmth drew people in, and whose heart remained true and steady.

Just like Simon, Mom was outgoing, magnetic, and overflowing with talent. She could dance with grace that seemed to make the air itself shimmer, paint scenes that captured light and emotion, write with a voice that stuck around long after the words were read, and craft anything her hands imagined. Her energy spilled over to everyone around her, lifting moods, inspiring smiles, and drawing people in effortlessly. She had a particular warmth for children, a gentle joy that made them feel seen and cherished.

In high school, she led the drill team as captain, moving with a precision and flair that turned every routine into a performance full of sparkle and vitality. When she danced, the room seemed to glow, as though light itself followed her steps. And when she smiled, her hazel eyes radiated warmth, lighting up every corner of the room. It was impossible not to notice her. Dad noticed her, of course. How could he not? He was captivated by her beauty and charm, utterly smitten. Their high school romance unfolded like a story written for them alone. They were inseparable, rarely seen apart, their laughter and companionship weaving a thread through those formative years that would carry them into the life they built together.

I remember those warm summer nights from my childhood, when the air in our living room seemed to hum with giggles and music. Mom would turn the music up, letting the beat take over, and she'd dance in the center of the room with Simon and me, twirling around her, our little feet barely keeping up with her energy. Dad would sway gently from his chair, a soft smile tugging at his lips as he watched us move.

Mom was determined to make our childhood sweet, to weave joy and light into our days, leaving behind memories that would last a lifetime. She wanted us to know happiness in its purest, simplest form, the kind that could carry us through the inevitable hardships of life. And sometimes, in those quiet moments of reflection, I found myself wishing I could tell her how deeply she succeeded. How her joy, her energy, and her love had shaped me, and how those memories still warmed my heart long after she was gone.

After college, Mom took a job in town as an elementary school teacher, bringing her boundless energy and big heart into every classroom. She had a special place in her heart for children who came from families struggling to make ends meet. Many of them were the sons and daughters of ranch workers, whose days were long and whose pockets were often empty. Ranching was good work, but it was rarely easy, and many of these kids faced challenges that extended far beyond the schoolyard.

Mom didn't stop at teaching. She volunteered with an organization dedicated to supporting underprivileged students, providing school supplies, mentoring, and even scholarships to help them pursue college or trade school. Her compassion and dedication left a mark that went far beyond the walls of the classroom.

After Simon and I were born, Mom shifted to part-time teaching to focus on raising us, but she continued to pour energy into her charity work. Her commitment never wavered, and over the years, she touched the lives of countless children, guiding them, encouraging them, and showing them that someone truly cared about their future. Her impact was quiet but profound, a ripple that reached far beyond what anyone could measure.

I was nothing like her. While Mom was outgoing, creative, and immersed in people, I was quiet and introspective, happiest when immersed in math problems or exploring the wonders of nature. She moved to the sounds of music and the brushstrokes of art, while I found joy in patterns, numbers, and the gentle curiosity of animals. Our interests couldn't have been more different, yet those differences never drove a wedge between us. If anything, they seemed to strengthen our bond, creating a bridge between two worlds that each valued the other's passions.

Mom always made sure I knew she was proud of me. She encouraged me to embrace who I truly was, to follow my own path, and to discover my purpose in life. Her smile, her quiet strength, and her unwavering love became my compass, guiding me through uncertainty and doubt. Even in the moments when I doubted myself, I carried her voice and her belief in me like a warm light, illuminating the way forward.

One of the greatest lessons my mom taught me was simple yet profound. God loved me. Her faith wasn't just words. It was the very foundation of who she was. She truly believed that God's love flowed through each of us, and her purpose in life was to be a vessel of that love, to share it freely with everyone she met.

Church was never optional in our house. Sundays were sacred, and even when icy roads made travel impossible, Mom made sure we still gathered in our living room, creating our own little sanctuary, our own service filled with song, prayer, and reflection. Her devotion extended beyond Sundays. Each morning at five, she would settle onto the couch under a cozy blanket, Bible open, coffee in hand, reading Scripture as the first light of day spilled across the room. Mom never preached in grand gestures or lofty words. She preached with her life, with quiet consistency, with the way she treated others, with the love she poured into her family and community. Life was not perfect. There were hardships, disappointments, and moments that would have shaken anyone else, but her faith never wavered. She shone through it all, a bright star in a sometimes dark world, and in her light, I learned the power of belief, love, and resilience.

Simon reminded me so much of her. He had that rare gift of making everyone feel seen, of walking into a room and somehow owning it without arrogance, just warmth. He was generous, always ready to lend a hand, and I can't recall us ever fighting the way most siblings do. Maybe it was because I was too quiet and shy, or maybe because he was simply too nice.

When he and my mom died, it wasn't just my world that shattered. It felt like the entire town ripped open. Their absence left a wound so deep, I didn't think the community would ever fully heal. They had left their mark, not in grand gestures, but in the steady, everyday ways they touched lives. My mom had spent years pouring herself into kids who needed her, and in them, her life would continue to ripple forward.

Sadly, my grandparents never found joy again. Losing their daughter and their grandson was a heartbreak too powerful to overcome. They did not live long after that. Soon, my mom's siblings and their families all moved far away, too. I rarely saw them or heard from them. It was not that they stopped loving me and my dad. It was just that they could not endure passing by that part of the road where their sister and nephew took their last breath. And when their parents died, it was the final blow. They had to go to avoid losing their sanity. Death is a monster that crushes lives beneath its dark shadow.

One of the few pieces of Mom's jewelry I still wear is her diamond tennis bracelet. She was never one for extravagance, but she adored that bracelet because it was the first piece of jewelry my dad ever bought her. And maybe it's only my imagination, but sometimes when I hold it close, it still smells faintly of her, vanilla, soft and sweet.

After Dad died, I discovered some of her artwork tucked carefully away in a drawer in his shop. He must have placed them there himself, as though keeping them safe until someone else was ready to see them again. I stored them in a storage unit in my hometown, too fragile for my grief at the time, promising myself that one day I'd frame them and hang them in my own home. Each brushstroke is a burst of joy, a kaleidoscope of color that feels like her laughter spilled onto canvas.

There will never be another like my mom. In quiet moments, I picture her walking heaven's golden streets with Jesus, pointing out colors only the two of them could dream up. Sometimes, I imagine them dancing together in the clouds, and my longing to join them nearly swallows me whole. But then I remember her lessons, that courage can be chosen, that love can outlast even death. I might not be as radiant as she was, but her light and love live on inside me, and I have learned, in my own way, to let them shine.

Crews

CHAPTER 15
Ring

There were moments when I realized just how fortunate I really was, wealthy in ways most people my age could hardly imagine. At twenty-two, I carried a quiet security that few of my peers knew, thanks to my dad's brother, Uncle Jeremy. He had carefully safeguarded my inheritance, tucking it away into a strong savings account that grew steadily. As an accountant, a field where numbers and discipline came naturally to me, I knew how to budget, how to plan, how to resist temptation. I wasn't a reckless spender. I enjoyed nice clothes, sure, but I wasn't extravagant. My money mostly sat untouched, a silent reassurance in the background of my life.

But one morning, I felt something stir inside me, a craving for more than just stability. My blue Toyota Camry had been with me since college, a loyal companion that never failed me, with excellent gas mileage and a reliability I could always count on. Still, every time I slid behind the wheel, I felt the sameness of routine. That morning, I decided it was time for something different, something that felt like a reward for all my careful choices. I opened my laptop, scrolled through listings, and there it was, a charcoal gray Lexus SUV, brand new, shimmering on the screen as if it had been waiting for me. It gleamed with leather seats, high-tech features, and luxuries I had never let myself even consider before.

On impulse, something wildly unlike me, I decided to buy it. No endless lists of pros and cons, no second-guessing. Just a sudden certainty. Within hours, I sold my Camry and signed the papers for the Lexus, my heart racing with every step. The dealership handed me the keys, and as I slid into the driver's seat, the smell of new leather wrapped around me like a big, comforting hug.

I had plans with my friend group that evening. I couldn't stop picturing the look on their faces when I pulled up in my sleek new SUV, headlights cutting through the dusk, engine humming. Driving away from the lot, I smiled to myself, hands gripping the wheel, thrilled not just by the purchase, but by the fact that, for once, I hadn't played it safe.

Daniel usually picked me up when we had plans, but that evening he couldn't. He was tied up at a golf tournament with his dad, so we agreed to meet directly at the restaurant. When I pulled into the lot, the first thing I noticed was his car already parked neatly under one of the lights. Right beside it sat Jackie's. Across the way, I spotted Todd and Stephanie pulling in, Todd behind the wheel like always. I waved through my windshield, and within seconds, they were crossing the lot toward me. Todd's eyes went wide the moment he saw the Lexus, his grin spreading as he picked up his pace.

"Whoa! This is yours?" he said, circling the vehicle like a kid in a candy shop. He ran his hand along the side, admiring every curve. "You've got to let me see the inside." I beamed, unlocking the door so he could peek in. Stephanie hung back a little, smiling but with that familiar hesitation she carried sometimes, the shadow of being the one in the group who didn't have much money. Still, she managed to shake it off, stepping closer to rest her hand lightly on the door. "It's really pretty," she said sincerely, her smile warming as she congratulated me. For a moment, I felt proud, even giddy.

The three of us walked inside together, the smell of sizzling fajitas filling the air. Daniel and Jackie were already at the table, mid-conversation, but Todd wasted no time blurting it out. "You guys have to see this. Callie just bought a brand-new Lexus! It's loaded, all the bells and whistles." His excitement made me blush, though Stephanie quickly added, "It really is beautiful." Jackie offered her congratulations with a bright, effortless smile.

Daniel, though, didn't speak right away. His eyes widened slightly, almost as if I'd just confessed something scandalous. After a pause, he rose from his chair and gave me a quick hug, the kind that felt polite but distant. "What sparked this?" he finally asked, his tone even but edged with surprise.

I shrugged lightly, trying to keep my voice casual. "The Camry was great, but it was getting older. I just wanted something new." But even as I said it, a familiar knot tightened in my stomach. His expression was hard to read, but I could feel it, that subtle air of judgment that seemed to hang between us more often than I wanted to admit. The pride I'd felt just moments earlier dimmed under the weight of it, leaving me squirming in my seat. Why was it that Daniel, of all people, so often managed to make me feel small, as if my choices, no matter how harmless, were something I needed to defend?

Dinner turned out to be lighthearted, thankfully. No one mentioned my SUV again, and I let myself relax, engaging in stories that bounced easily around the table. By the time we stepped outside, the evening air was cool, carrying the faint hum of traffic from the street. That's when the attention turned back to me.

Naturally, everyone drifted toward the new Lexus. Todd's enthusiasm flared all over again. He practically pressed his face against the glass, marveling at the dashboard lights. Jackie hung back a little, her arms crossed, but her smile kind. "It really is nice, Callie," she said, her tone simple but genuine.

One by one, the group began saying their goodbyes, peeling off toward their own cars until it was just Daniel and me standing side by side in the lot. My SUV loomed quietly between us, shining under the yellow glow of the overhead lamps. Daniel's gaze stayed on it for a moment before he turned to me. "Can I get inside?" he asked. I nodded, handing him the keys without hesitation. He slipped into the driver's seat, adjusting it instinctively, while I climbed into the passenger side. For a moment, the new-car smell wrapped around us like something intimate and intoxicating. He started the engine, its low, smooth hum filling the silence, then eased the car out of the space and steered it around the block.

But he said nothing. Not a single word. The quiet pressed

heavier with each turn of the wheel, until the excitement I'd felt earlier from Todd's praise was replaced by a thick unease. By the time we returned, parking neatly beside his own car, Daniel killed the engine and sat still, his hands resting on the wheel. When he finally spoke, his voice was calm, almost too calm. "Callie, why would you go and buy something like this? Were you alone? How do you even know you got a good deal? Why wouldn't you ask me to come with you? And, why do you need something so expensive?"

Each question landed like a pebble dropped into water, rippling into something sharper. My chest tightened. It wasn't curiosity. It was an interrogation. Why did I always have to defend myself with him? Why was every choice I made dissected, as though I couldn't be trusted to know what was best for me?

Sitting there in the dim parking lot, I realized Daniel truly had no idea about the depth of my wealth. He'd caught glimpses, of course, of me buying dinner without a second thought, surprising him with gifts that cost more than most people in their twenties would dare spend, never once complaining about money the way the others do. But he didn't know. Not really.

So I told him. I did not go into detail, and I chose my words carefully. My voice was quiet, steady. "I don't talk about this much, Daniel, but I do have money."

His jaw tightened instantly, lips pressed into a thin line. Those eyes went dark again. I saw envy, anger, maybe even fear, and for a second, it made the space between us feel wide. I swallowed and went on, forcing myself to meet his stare. "Look, I don't waste money. I don't spend just to spend. But I wanted a new car. This one is safe, it's reliable, and I like it. That's all." But the words hung heavy in the silence that followed, and the look on Daniel's face told me this wasn't going to be as simple as I wanted it to be.

For a while after that night, things between Daniel and me smoothed over. We laughed more, argued less, and on the surface, it felt as though the awkwardness about the Lexus had faded. But the cracks were still there, waiting.

The most jarring moment came at his parents' dinner table a couple of weeks later. We were halfway through a meal when Daniel suddenly blurted out, "Did you know that Callie is rich?"

The words hit me like a slap. Conversation halted, forks hovered in midair, and every pair of eyes turned toward me. My chest tightened as heat crept up my neck. Daniel wasn't finished. "She bought a brand-new Lexus SUV," he added, his voice carrying more pride than warmth, "with every upgrade you can imagine."

A strained silence followed before his parents offered polite congratulations, their smiles thin and unreadable. Leslie, who was visiting that evening, echoed them cheerfully, but I could feel something else in the air, something sharp. Instead of admiration, it felt like judgment. I sat there, shifting uncomfortably under their gaze, trying to understand why my purchase seemed to bother them. These were people who surrounded themselves with golden chandeliers, imported rugs, and a dining room that looked like it belonged in the pages of a magazine. They spent lavishly on possessions, flaunting a lifestyle of ease. Shouldn't they, of all people, appreciate a beautiful new car?

But they didn't. Or maybe they couldn't. And that was when I began to sense it, that subtle schism in the atmosphere, like a hairline crack running through porcelain. Was their abundance real, or was it performance? Did Daniel's family actually live in the wealth they displayed, or was it all carefully constructed, a facade meant to convince the world of something that wasn't entirely true? The question lodged itself deep in my mind, and once it was there, I couldn't stop turning it over.

I began to replay scenes from the past few months like clips from a film I hadn't realized I was watching too closely. The extravagant Christmas gifts wrapped in glittering paper. The immaculate nails and hair, always styled as if for a fashion magazine spread. The expensive furniture in a sprawling house that seemed almost too perfect, too staged. Was it possible the Masters weren't as financially secure as they appeared? Were they drowning in debt, putting on a performance of wealth for the world to admire?

And then there was Daniel. His car was fine, nothing remarkable, just decent. He lived with two roommates in a modest apartment, not luxurious by any measure, though nice enough. Still, he carried himself with a certain pride, almost a rehearsed polish. When he introduced himself to others, I noticed how carefully he phrased it, "I'm at the Hutchins & Beard Law Firm." He never clarified that he was a paralegal. He let people assume, perhaps even encouraged them to believe, that he was something more, an attorney, someone climbing the ranks. It made me wonder. Was Daniel also performing?

And what of his parents? His father, with his booming

voice and expensive watch, worked in sales for a medical supply company. From the outside, it seemed like a lucrative field. Annette managed human resources at a lumber company. Respectable, steady work. They behaved like a family of means. They looked the part, dressed the part, lived in a house that certainly seemed the part. But the more I thought about it, the more a strange feeling crept in. Maybe it was all surface-level gloss, a veneer of affluence stretched thin over something far less glamorous. Maybe everything they presented to the world was just an act.

Money was never the center of my world. It wasn't something I obsessed over or flaunted, and it certainly never defined who I was. My parents weren't billionaires by any stretch, but they worked tirelessly, made smart choices, and invested wisely. Because of them, I grew up with security, a kind of quiet abundance that allowed me to live without constantly worrying about what things cost. My father left me everything upon his death, but even before that, I never had to think much about money. It was simply there, steady and dependable, like a current running beneath our lives.

But what I valued most was that we never lived like we were trying to prove anything. We didn't overspend, we didn't flash wealth, and we never used it to measure our worth. My mom believed money should move outward, not inward. She taught me generosity as if it were a second language. I think my parents gave away more throughout their lifetime than they ever spent on themselves, and they did it quietly, without fanfare. That was the example set for me, to see money not as a crown or shield, but as a tool for kindness, for helping, for building something good.

At the end of May, Daniel invited me to dinner at a French restaurant, one of those elegant, candlelit places you only ever pass by and wonder about. He told me to dress up, to make the night feel special, and my heart leapt at the thought.

That morning, Jackie called to ask if I wanted to join her at the nail salon. I said yes, and while we sat side by side in those oversized chairs, she leaned over with a grin. "Since you're going to a French restaurant, why not go classic? French tips? Simple, but elegant."

I laughed because manicures weren't really me. I was a country girl through and through. My hands were more familiar with dirt, hay, and animal stalls than glossy polish. Still, every so often, I liked the indulgence of something delicate and feminine. So, I agreed. By the time I left, the soft pink with white tips made me smile every time I glanced down at my hands.

Things with Daniel had been smooth lately, easier than they'd been in weeks. He had even grown fond of my SUV, asking to drive it whenever we went out. It made me feel as though we were finding our rhythm again. That evening, he came to my apartment and parked out front. I buzzed him in, and when I opened the door, the sight of him stole my breath. He was wearing a dark suit, sharp and tailored, his beard trimmed neatly and his hair slicked back, the style drawing out the rugged line of his jaw. His eyes caught mine, carrying a light that reached straight through me, and in that moment, I couldn't imagine looking anywhere else.

Before I could even speak, he pulled me into his arms, his lips finding mine in a kiss that made the world around me dissolve. My body melted against his, every defense slipping away. I could have stayed suspended in that moment forever. But then he pulled back just enough to look at me, his mouth curving into a smile. "You are beautiful," he said softly. And I was melting all over again, helpless against the warmth that spread through me.

We climbed into the Lexus and he drove us to the restaurant. We had an easy conversation, and the night seemed extra beautiful as the city lights filled the air with color. When we arrived, hopped out, and handed the key to the valet, Daniel took one more look at me and smiled, "I hope you remember this night forever."

We stepped through the restaurant doors, and before I could take in the scent of roasted garlic and wine, my eyes landed on the bar area just a few feet inside. A cluster of balloons floated above candles, casting a warm glow across a gathering of familiar faces. His parents. His sisters and brother-in-law. Jackie, Stephanie, and Todd. All of them stood together beneath a massive banner stretched across the wall that read, "Calista, will you marry me?"

My knees went weak. The room tilted ever so slightly, as if the ground beneath me wasn't solid anymore. Every head in the restaurant turned, every pair of eyes narrowing in on me. I could feel their stares pressing into my skin, tightening the air around me. Attention has never been something I sought. I've always been happiest on the edges of a room, not at its center. But suddenly I was a spectacle, the star of a scene that seemed designed for everyone but me.

And then I turned. Daniel was no longer by my side. He was kneeling on one knee, a velvet box open in his hand, the sparkle of the ring catching the candlelight. His voice, rich and steady, rose above the hush of the restaurant. "Callie, will you do me the honor of being my wife?"

My heart fluttered in my chest. My body felt shaky as though I might collapse under the weight of so many eyes and expectations. Jackie held her phone up, recording every second, her smile wide and eager. Stephanie and Todd stood close together, grinning. His family's gazes were sharp, hungry, waiting for my answer. The entire restaurant, strangers and loved ones alike, leaned into the moment.

I swallowed hard, a tear sliding down my cheek before I could stop it. "Yes," I whispered, my voice trembling but certain enough to be heard. Daniel's face broke into a grin as he rose swiftly to his feet, scooping me up into his arms as applause erupted around us. His lips found mine in a kiss that sealed the moment, while cheers and clapping filled the restaurant. To everyone else, it was the perfect fairytale ending. But deep inside, beneath the rush of noise and the shimmer of the ring on my finger, I still felt that unease, that strange awareness of so many eyes, so much performance, and the nagging sense that this wasn't just our moment. It belonged to everyone else, too.

I stepped out of all the noise for a moment and into the quiet of the night. My fingers trembled as I dialed Grandma's number. She should have been here. Had Daniel even told her? When she answered, her voice was thin, weary, as though pulled from a restless sleep. "Grandma," I whispered, "I have some news."

I told her I was engaged, bracing myself for the warmth of her blessing, the reassurance I desperately needed, that I had made the right choice. But instead, her response was muted, her tone neither joyful nor sorrowful. Just tired. Perhaps even confused. Our words were brief, and before long, I promised I would call her the next day. I told myself she must have been half-asleep, not grasping the moment, not realizing the weight of it.

Inside, the night burned bright with celebration. Daniel's parents had bought dinner for everyone, and the air buzzed with clinking glasses and eager chatter. Daniel glowed with pride, showing off the ring as friends and family crowded in to admire it. It was larger than anything I would have chosen for myself, too big, too loud, but undeniably beautiful. Under the lights, it glittered fiercely, sparkling like the champagne we raised in toasts.

When the night finally ended, Daniel kissed me long and deep, leaving me with a playful, "See you tomorrow, future Mrs. Masters." Alone in my room, I slipped into my pajamas, curled beneath the covers, and lifted my hand one more time. The manicure was perfect. The ring was dazzling.

CHAPTER 16
Quicksand

I sat alone on the bench in my courtyard, the warm air wrapping around me as I replayed the last nine months of my life. What a whirlwind it had been. Too much, too fast. I had moved to a new city, buried my father, fallen for a man, and now, an engagement ring glittered on my hand. The sheer absurdity of it crashed over me, and with it came a wave of shame. What was I doing? Who was I becoming?

I began to question the very thing I thought I understood. Love. Not the love I had always known, the steady, unquestionable kind. Love had been my family gathered around a kitchen table or dancing on the front porch. Love had been my childhood home on the ranch, with stars so bright they seemed to sing. Love had been God's presence, constant and sure. But this? This romantic kind? I realized I was a novice, fumbling in the dark.

In high school, I had danced with boys and laughed through awkward dates, but never had a true boyfriend. In college, most of my dates were in groups, with a few scattered dinners here and there. Steve, the shy, nerdy guy from my accounting class, was one. I remembered the awkwardness of his one attempted kiss, how we both pulled away and agreed on friendship instead. Then there was Scott, charming, easy to be with. His kisses had been light, sweet, almost innocent. Pleasant, but not like Daniel's. Daniel's kisses had weight, urgency, fire.

Unlike so many girls I knew, I had never been one to lose myself in a boy. And yet, deep down, a longing had always burned in me to fall deeply in love, to marry, to build a family on a ranch. A life as simple and beautiful as the one my parents had given me.

So why had I convinced myself I loved Daniel? And what proof had I ever truly had that he loved me? Looking back now, the answer is clearer than it ever was then. Grief drove me. When Dad died, I was a shell. I was lonely, desperate for warmth to fill the big hole in my heart. I hadn't gone searching for Daniel, but we found each other. He reached out first, and in my brokenness, I clung.

I remember the very first man I noticed after moving to the city, the one I bumped into in the hall. Tall, striking, with piercing green eyes. I had run into my apartment that day with a girlish wish that someday I might marry someone who looked like him. Daniel didn't look like that man, but he filled something deep inside me. He soothed my raw edges, gave me attention when I was aching for it most, and for a while, he made me feel safe, even cherished.

In those first months, his kisses were everything. Sweet honey, intoxicating. I craved them like water in a desert, like

I had never craved anything before. And maybe that was the truth of it. I wasn't in love with Daniel. I was in love with the comfort he provided, and with the way his lips could make me forget, if only for a moment, the gaping wound of loss.

And what about Daniel? Why did he believe he was in love with me? At first, he showered me with praise, lifting me up with kind words and gentle encouragement. But the moment the criticism began, the mask slipped, and I glimpsed the truth of his thoughts. Then, just as quickly, he would pull me back in, smothering me with affection so sweet and overwhelming that I forgot the sting of his lectures. Yet beneath it all was the constant refrain. Change. Change this, change that. Always shaping, always molding. But how can you truly love someone if you cannot love them as they are? Daniel didn't love me. He loved an image, a woman he wished I could become.

And a sharp question pierced me, "Was I guilty of the same? Did I love Daniel, or did I only love the way he filled my emptiness, the role he played in my story of grief and longing? Were we fooling ourselves, pretending this was love, binding ourselves with an engagement neither of us fully understood?"

When she saw my ring, Katie squealed with delight. "Chica, that's a rock!" she exclaimed, her laughter bright and effortless. My coworkers gathered, buzzing with questions about the proposal, planning showers and celebrations as though love was nothing more than a checklist of events. Their joy pressed around me like confetti. But Paul stood apart. He offered his congratulations, yes, but his eyes carried something heavier. Concern. A quiet warning I wasn't quite ready to hear.

The days that followed blurred into a whirl of commotion. Friends, Daniel's family, and nearly everyone in his wide circle buzzed with plans for engagement parties and showers. Invitations, decorations, menus. It seemed there was no end to the excitement. And yet, in the midst of all that noise, I felt the silence of my own circle. I hadn't spoken to anyone from my life back home, except Grandma.

That first night, she had sounded distant, almost disoriented, her words thin and unsettled. But when I called again the next day, she seemed more like herself. She told me she was happy for me, and then, with a catch in her voice, she said she wished my parents and Simon were here to see it all. The depth of that loss struck us both, sharp and merciless. Still, we happily talked on the phone about the proposal, about plans for the future. And then, as the conversation drew to a close, her voice softened into a question that stilled me. "Callie, dear, do you love Daniel? Is he the one?"

Something in her tone lodged itself in me. Did I love him? Was he the one? I searched my heart, and all I found was uncertainty. Once, I had believed in the idea of a soul meant just for you. I had seen it in my parents, the way they fit so effortlessly together, two halves of one whole. But now I wasn't so sure. Perhaps that kind of love was rare, a miracle reserved for only a few. Perhaps it was something I was never meant to have.

Daniel was almost giddy. The first thing he did was log onto social media, eager to announce our engagement to the world. Every "like," every heart, every congratulatory comment seemed to fuel him, and he devoured them hungrily. He turned to me again and again, asking, "What do you think of the ring?" Each time, I gave the same answer. It was beautiful, and I thanked him. Yet beneath his enthusiasm, I wondered if he was celebrating the proposal itself more than the marriage it was supposed to promise.

Had he thought beyond the parties, the ring, the photographs? Shouldn't we be meeting with a minister, sitting down in premarital counseling, asking hard questions about our future? I longed to talk about the practical things. Finances, where we would live, children, how we would build a life together. But Daniel brushed all that aside. He wanted the glow of the present, the thrill of the moment, the sparkle without the weight.

I sifted through memories of our many dates, trying to recall when we had talked deeply about anything that truly mattered. In my mind, I had believed our time together brimmed with conversation, but now a darker truth pressed in. We had never gone deep at all. We had skimmed the surface. We had not spoken of faith, of convictions, of the world around us, of money, or children, or the shape of a shared life.

And suddenly, with a cold clarity, I realized I didn't really know Daniel. He didn't really know me. And the pieces of me he did glimpse, he wanted to change. A knot of dread coiled in my stomach. I began to truly worry.

But I played along. I became the blushing bride who giggled like a schoolgirl over bridal magazines and lost herself in the endless scroll of Pinterest boards. I sipped champagne while Jackie and Stephanie planned the parties and color palettes. I posed again and again in carefully staged snapshots beside Daniel so his mom and sisters could curate the perfect image of our engagement for the world to see. I smiled. I laughed. I sparkled like the rock on my finger, like the star they all wanted me to be.

But beneath that polished glow, a shadow lurked. Inside my heart, there was no glitter, only a quiet ache where certainty should have been. I was performing a happiness I could not quite feel, wrapped in satin and smiles, yet stumbling somewhere in the dark.

Daniel and I rarely spent time alone during all the commotion. I craved quiet, unhurried hours with the man I was about to marry. I wanted to really see him, to truly know him before we crossed that threshold together. Yet while I was searching for depth, he seemed content with the surface. We were diving headfirst into marriage, but his eyes stayed fixed on the immediate fun of it all.

Isn't it supposed to be the other way around? Men are said to be the practical ones, the planners, the steady hands steering the future. Women are the dreamers, the ones enchanted by the sparkle of the ring, lost in the froth of tulle and lace, caught up in the giddiness of the moment. But here I was, standing still and searching for something real while he, it seemed, was already lost in the show.

Show. That was what Daniel and his family wanted. My eyes began to open, slowly at first, like dawn creeping into a darkened room, and then with startling clarity. They were masters at performance, seamless pageantry, curated smiles, the sheen of effortless perfection. Their world sparkled on the outside. Rich, talented, attractive, enviable. But inside, it was empty, a shell stretched over something weary and fractured. The Masters didn't live life. They staged it. And once I was engaged to Daniel, I was ushered backstage, where the lights didn't reach and the cracks showed plainly.

Annette, forever gracious in public, dulled her quiet despair with daily prescriptions. Bob, the patriarch with a firm handshake and louder laugh, spent his life either buried in work or lost on the golf course. Amanda and Jason's marriage was a battlefield of sharp words and cold silences. Some nights, Amanda fled to her parents' house just to escape the smoke of their latest skirmish. Leslie was the one who haunted me most. Poised and stoic on the outside, but with something restless and dark simmering beneath the surface. I couldn't name it at first, but over time, the shadow behind her smile became clearer. Pain left untreated, wounds never allowed to heal. Jenna confided in me one quiet afternoon, her voice low, telling me how Leslie had been assaulted in high school and had never sought the help she needed. Instead, she built walls of fury and guardedness, armor against a world that had betrayed her.

It wasn't just the outside world that had betrayed her. It was her own flesh and blood. The people who were supposed to hold her pain with care, to help her carry the weight of what had happened, had instead demanded silence. They wanted her to smile through the cracks, to press her trauma into a neat little box and shove it to the back of the closet where no one would ever have to see it. Leslie learned how to play her part in the family's theater, how to smile just wide enough for the camera, how to answer questions without revealing the torment in her voice. Annette and Bob curated their lives like a gallery, each family photo framed with precision, each smile polished until it gleamed with the illusion of perfection. On those walls, nothing was broken, nothing was missing, nothing hurt.

Jenna was the only one who seemed untouched by the family's suffocating script. College had given her room to breathe, to become someone real, someone freer. Of them all, she had a chance to escape the stage. I found myself silently rooting for her to run far, build a life filled with real friends, real joy, far away from the velvet curtains and painted sets. And then, of course, there was Daniel. A leading man in this carefully lit production. As the curtain drew back, I began to see the threads of his truth too, unraveling slowly, but undeniably.

One early evening, I sat curled in Daniel's recliner, waiting for him to finish getting ready for our dinner with the group. The apartment was quiet except for the distant rush of the shower, and my eyes wandered, idly at first, until they caught on a small box of papers on the floor. A sliver of pink was slipping out from the corner, about to fall. I reached down to tuck it back in, but the moment I pulled it free, my pulse caught. It was a receipt for my engagement ring. The words blurred for a moment as I scanned them, but there it was in bold type, "Round cut Moissanite engagement ring."

Moissanite? I didn't even know what that was. The price, just over two thousand dollars, stared back at me, small and unassuming beneath the weight of the stone I wore. I had wondered, quietly, how Daniel could have afforded a ring that looked like it belonged in a jeweler's vault. I pulled out my phone and typed the word. "A rare mineral used as a durable, affordable, and sparkling alternative to diamonds, different chemical composition, more pronounced rainbow-colored fire."

There it was. Not a diamond. Not what it appeared to be. I looked down at the massive rock on my finger, the symbol of his love, his future, his promise, and I saw the truth. The ring was just like the family, brilliant on the surface, but in the light, the colors fractured, revealing something cheaper, something fake.

I struggled with whether or not I should confront Daniel, the receipt burning a hole in my palm like a secret I never asked to keep. It wasn't about the stone. I had never dreamt of wearing a rock that size. That kind of flash was never my style. It wasn't even about money. It was about what the ring represented or, more accurately, what it concealed. A promise built on a lie. Would Daniel have ever told me? Or had he planned to let me wear that sparkly facade for the rest of my life, smiling proudly while strangers admired the illusion? And if he was willing to lie about something so symbolic, what else was he hiding?

By the time he stepped out of his room, hair still damp from the shower, buttoning his shirt, my decision was made. I held the receipt out like evidence. My voice barely wavered. "Is my ring fake?"

For a heartbeat, he froze, blank, unreadable. Then his eyes darkened, and his jaw tightened. "What are you doing going through my things?" he snapped, his voice sharp enough to cut. That moment chilled me. Not because of the ring, but because I saw something in him I hadn't fully seen before. Defensiveness that twisted into anger, and anger that twisted into blame. We fought. Not a spat, not a lovers' quarrel, but a storm. The yelling climbed the walls, so fierce I half-expected a knock from the neighbors. He shouted about privacy and betrayal, but I stood my ground. For once, I did not shrink. I matched his voice, my throat raw from the effort, because this wasn't about a shiny stone anymore. It was about truth.

"Tell me the truth about you. About money. About our future," I demanded, my voice shaking, but strong enough to stand. Dinner plans were forgotten. He texted the group that something had come up and we wouldn't make it. The hours dragged on, the tension thick as tar, until finally, his fury deflated into something closer to defeat. And then the truth tumbled out.

He was drowning. They all were. His parents had mortgaged their home twice, juggling debts they could no longer control. His sisters, his brother-in-law, even Daniel himself, were buried in loans, credit cards, and promises they couldn't keep. Daniel's charming, confident facade was built on quicksand, and the ring was just another prop in their family performance.

CHAPTER 17
Falling

The summer months brought a heat that clung to the skin, heavy and relentless. Daniel and I wavered through it, our relationship a pendulum swinging between uneasy peace and sharp, silent rifts. Yet somehow, we stayed engaged. We even set a date. October, just before my birthday, as if a calendar could bind together what our hearts hadn't fully secured.

After uncovering the truth about his debt, I made a decision. I would help pay it off. It felt like the only way forward, the only way to level the ground between us. And in that decision, I revealed my own secret. I told him fully about my inheritance, the exact amount. If I demanded his honesty, I had to offer mine. His reaction frightened me. There was a flicker of shame in his eyes, a shadow of embarrassment over our starkly different financial realities. But there was something else too, something brighter, almost electric. Excitement. Thrill. Hunger.

Soon, he began speaking in a language that made my

stomach turn. He needed a new car. "We" should probably purchase it before the wedding. We. That word, so small and binding, cut deep. Was it really "we," or was it me? Would my money become his by default before vows were ever exchanged? The balance of my life felt off-kilter, the scales tipping in ways I couldn't quite fix. The heat outside mirrored the slow burn within me, unrest, doubt, and a longing that gnawed at my chest.

In June, we drove to see my grandma. She saw the ring (oh, that ring) and her face lit with questions about our plans. She hugged us both so tightly, her embrace soft yet desperate, as though holding on to something slipping away. And when I was in her arms, I didn't want to let go. I didn't want to get back into my SUV or return to the city that had slowly been draining me. I wanted to stay. To come home. But even home was changing. Grandma moved slower, spoke slower. Her hands, once so steady, trembled. Her mind was fading. She was all the family I had left, and I could feel time stealing her from me.

By July, I was worn thin, like fabric that had been pulled too many times in too many directions. One evening, I was thrown a lifeline. My college roommate Jennifer called. We hadn't spoken in ages, but the moment I heard her voice, it felt like slipping back into a soft, familiar sweater. She was glowing, even over the phone, and I could hear it in her tone. Pregnant and in her second trimester, she spoke of her growing belly with a mixture of awe and humor. Her husband, buried in a mountain of work, had suggested she take a trip before the sleepless nights and diaper days began. "One last adventure," she said. And then came the invitation.

Would I join her? It wasn't just any getaway. It was Italy.

The very word felt like a deep breath, like cool water poured over a parched soul. I had been to Europe once before with my dad, Germany, Austria, Switzerland. Those days were tucked into my memory like pressed flowers in a book. Fragrant, colorful, impossibly precious. The thought of returning to that continent, to beauty and history and something so far from my current storm, was intoxicating. And so, without hesitation, I said yes.

Ten days of freedom followed. Ten days of Rome's golden sunsets and the rolling hills of Tuscany. We ate pasta that tasted like it had been kissed by the sun. We toured museums where marble saints and emperors watched us pass. We stood beneath the vastness of the Vatican dome, whispered under the arches of the Colosseum, and I sipped wine in vineyards that looked like paintings while Jennifer drank grape juice.

Our nights were alive with music spilling from the streets near the Spanish Steps. We threw coins into the Trevi Fountain, one for a wish, one for a prayer, one for courage. We laughed until our cheeks ached. We played like girls who had never carried burdens. And in that rare space of lightness, I opened my heart. One night, sitting by a fountain, the cool stone beneath us and the hum of foreign voices around, I told her everything. About Daniel. About the criticism that cut deeper than he realized. About the family that sparkled like glass but felt just as fragile. And finally, the secret I had told no one, that the ring was fake and that its weight signified so much more than words could express.

Jennifer listened, not with judgment, not with gasps, just a calm, patient stillness that wrapped around me like a blanket. She held me when my voice cracked. She looked me in the eyes, and for a moment, I saw in her the same kind of steady, grounding love that Katie once gave me "Listen to your heart, Cal," she said softly, "but also listen to your brain. If you feel even the faintest tingle of doubt, you owe it to yourself to pay attention. Doubt isn't always the enemy. It's often the warning sign before the storm." In that quiet Roman night, something inside me stirred. I wasn't ready to name it yet. But it was there.

When I returned from Europe, I carried with me something I hadn't felt in a long time, lightness. My skin still held the kiss of the Tuscan sun, and my mind was clearer than it had been in months. My heart was still tangled, but at least it was breathing again. I slipped back into work with a quiet determination. The familiar hum of my office kept my mind occupied. I adored the updates on baby Brady, each photo a reminder that life, even in its chaos, could create something so tender and new. I made a small ritual of bringing James his daily coffee, watching him fight through the exhaustion of sleepless nights with a grateful half-smile.

And then there was Katie, floating on her own little cloud of joy. She had met a man, Christian, and the way she said his name, almost like a melody, told me everything. One afternoon, he joined us for lunch. Christian wasn't loud, but he was warm, open, the kind of man who seemed to draw people toward him rather than command their attention. His charm was effortless, his kindness genuine. He matched Katie's effervescence without trying to outshine it, a spark meeting a flame and burning steadily side by side. Watching them, I felt that bittersweet ache in my chest, the one that comes when you see what you hope love could be while realizing you don't have it. Katie was falling hard and fast, and I was truly happy for her.

My friends threw themselves into planning with the kind of enthusiasm that left little room for silence. There were constant conversations about showers, bachelor and bachelorette parties, and endless little details. Jackie and Stephanie decided on a girls' trip to a nearby winery, inviting a few women from our Bible study, my future sisters-in-law, and Katie. They had only met Katie a handful of times, but Stephanie seemed to warm to her quickly, laughing easily at her stories. Jackie, on the other hand, kept a polite distance, her smile tight, her tone clipped. Katie, being Katie, lighthearted, carefree, the eternal party chica, never let it bother her. She floated above the tension as if it couldn't touch her.

Meanwhile, the larger wedding plans were beginning to take shape. The venue had already been chosen, an outdoor chapel perched on a hill near the Masters' home. It was undeniably beautiful, all rustic wood and wide, sweeping views, but it wasn't the simplicity I had envisioned for myself. Annette made it clear that she and her daughters would take charge of the planning since, as she reminded me, I didn't have a mother to do it. The words might have sounded compassionate, perhaps even generous to an outsider, but the truth was, they carried a sting.

I wanted something small, something intimate and meaningful, just a gathering of people who loved us. But small and simple didn't fit the Masters' image. Their world revolved around appearances, and appearances demanded spectacle. The wedding, I realized, would be another performance, another stage where I was less the bride and more the leading actress in someone else's production. Wait. Was I the leading actress or more in a supporting role?

The weight of it pressed on me as I sat through their chatter about floral arches, elaborate menus, and string quartets. For the first time, the reality of my aloneness cut through sharply. If ever a girl needed her mom, it was now. Instead, I was left trying to imagine Annette as mine, with Amanda, Leslie, and Jenna as my sisters. The thought of Jenna softened me. Her presence had always been kind, her sweetness authentic. But when I thought of the rest, my stomach twisted. I smiled when expected, nodded in the right places, but beneath it all was the harsh reality of knowing this was the family I was marrying into. And it didn't feel like home.

And then there was the discussion of funding. Daniel told his family about the depth of my inheritance. He had already told them that I was rich when I bought the SUV, but now that he knew the extent of my wealth, and now that we were engaged, he felt that he and his family were owed a share in it. Without hesitation, without my permission, he laid bare something I had guarded carefully, something private. Worse, he told them I intended to pay off his debts once we were married, and that together we would step into a life of ease, including new cars, a beautiful home, all the comforts he believed would fall into place the moment I became his wife.

I had made it clear to him more than once that I wouldn't

touch my inheritance until after the wedding. Still, he pressed. Sometimes gently, sometimes with irritation sharp enough to sting. He'd complain about his car breaking down and suggest I should buy him one, since I could. Other times, he grew angry, accusing me of dragging my feet, of not really wanting to marry him if I wasn't ready to "share" my money. Each accusation chipped away at me, leaving a painful mark where my excitement should have been.

Why didn't I run? Why didn't I gather the strength to walk away then and there? Instead, I stayed, even as the planning grew heavier. Annette announced that she and her daughters would take care of all the details, that my role, as she put it, was simply "to pay the bills and look pretty." The words landed like chains around my wrists, binding me to a wedding that did not feel like mine. I smiled when I was expected to, nodded when I was told to, all the while drowning in the quiet realization that I was being absorbed into their world, a world where my voice didn't matter, but my money certainly did.

At the end of summer, Jackie, Stephanie, and Katie joined me for what should have been one of the most exciting days of my life. Wedding dress shopping. In my heart, I longed to go home and step into a gown with Grandma by my side, to share something simple and sacred in the familiarity of my hometown. But Jackie insisted the city offered better choices, promising me there was a boutique downtown unlike any other.

What she hadn't told me was that the moment I walked in, I'd be ambushed. Annette, Amanda, Leslie, and Jenna were already there, glasses of champagne in hand, waiting like an audience. Their smiles were polished, their eyes bright with expectation. It was supposed to feel festive, but all I felt was cornered. Jackie and Katie fluttered around the racks, pulling gowns and holding them up against me, while Stephanie offered gentle suggestions in the background. Finally, we narrowed it down to four. They placed them in my arms and ushered me toward the fitting room as though I were on a stage about to perform.

Inside the little room, away from their chatter, I let the silence settle. I slipped into the first gown, its fabric whispering as it fell around me, heavy and elegant. For a moment, I stood still, staring at my reflection. The lace clung perfectly, the skirt fanned just so. Everything a bride should want. But as I studied myself, a sudden, sharp ache rose in my chest. My throat tightened. I wanted to cry. I wanted my mom.

I wanted to open the door and see her seated there with the others, champagne glass in hand, her hazel eyes sparkling with delight. I wanted her gentle nod of approval, her laughter filling the room, her presence reminding me I wasn't alone. My mind drifted to memories of her dancing, graceful, radiant, full of light. And the way she carried goodness like it was her very skin. I closed my eyes, trying to hold her close in my imagination, but it only made the sting stronger. All I craved was one quiet moment with her, one chance to share the joy every daughter dreams of. To have her squeeze my hand, to hear her voice as I rang a little bell and whispered through tears, "Yes to the dress." But when I opened my eyes, it was only me in the mirror. And outside, they were waiting.

To great applause, I stepped out in the third gown, and the room erupted with delight. Compliments overlapped. Jackie clapping, Katie's playful whistle, Annette pressing her hand to her chest as though she were overcome with emotion. Amanda and Leslie leaned in for a closer look, nodding in approval, and Jenna smiled wide and said, "You will be the most beautiful bride, Sis."

I turned before the mirror, the silk catching the light like water. It wasn't what I had ever envisioned for myself, but it was breathtaking, undeniably so. And for a moment, as the skirt swirled around my feet, I let myself feel it. I felt pretty.

The stylist circled me with quick precision, pins between her lips as she tucked and marked and measured. Champagne glasses clinked in the background, their laughter ringing out like a celebration. I smiled, nodded, and laughed when I was supposed to, letting their energy sweep me along. The dress was chosen, the box neatly ticked, and everyone left the boutique convinced we had shared a perfect afternoon.

But as the doors closed behind us and we stepped back into the late-summer sun, a heaviness pressed on me. The applause still boomed in my ears, loud and insistent, as though I had been performing. I had a dress, a beautiful gown that drew every eye and sealed every approval. Yet, beneath the shimmer of satin and the cheers, I felt the tug of something else, like a warning, like a whisper that my life was no longer mine.

As fall approached and the wedding date crept closer, the weight on my chest grew heavier with each passing day. Showers were held in our honor, packages stacked neatly on my doorstep, gifts arriving from our carefully curated registry. At least, it was their registry, filled with items Annette and Amanda had picked, insisting they knew what Daniel and I "really needed." Invitations were mailed to more than two hundred guests. Two hundred! I had wanted something small and quiet, something intimate and true. Instead, I found myself financing a grand production that felt like a big show, not a union of hearts.

The bills came in waves, large deposits, endless receipts. Every decision was made without me, except when it came time to pay. Daniel's family had agreed to cover just one thing, the honeymoon. I had dreamed of mountains, of cool air and quiet mornings, maybe a firelit cabin where we could breathe and be still. Daniel wanted the Caribbean. And just like that, Annette and Bob purchased tickets to the Bahamas. Their choice, his choice, never mine. I was the bride, yet I felt more like a guest of honor at a show designed by someone else. Every ribbon tied, every flower ordered, every song chosen, all without me. My only role, it seemed, was to sign checks and smile.

By late September, my bachelorette trip was planned. Jackie and Stephanie had arranged for a weekend at a winery two hours away, complete with wine tastings and shopping excursions. On paper, it sounded lovely. In truth, it felt like one more box checked off a list that wasn't mine. The air that weekend was crisp, the trees dressed in shades of gold and rust, the kind of beauty that usually lifted my spirit. But I could not shake the dread coiling tighter inside me. I laughed when expected, posed for photos with a glass of wine in hand, but behind the practiced smile, I was crumbling. I was falling. And the most terrifying question of all whispered at the edges of my thoughts, "Would I ever be able to get back up?"

Crews

CHAPTER 18
Wedding Chapel

At the very edge of my hometown, where the dirt roads wound beneath the shade of towering oaks and maples, there stood an old wedding chapel. Perched on a gentle hill, its white steeple catching the sunlight, it watched over decades of vows made and kept. My mom and dad were married there, and throughout my life, I'd sat in its worn wooden pews for more weddings than I could count.

The chapel was weathered in the loveliest way. Its paint was softened by summers of heat and winters of ice. There was a peace about it, a humility, a kind of quiet magic that made you believe promises made there might actually hold. Just beyond it stood the big red barn, once a working relic of the land, now draped in string lights and polished wood, a place where joyful laughter boomed, glasses clinked, and new husbands twirled their brides across the floor.

I loved that chapel, not for its beauty, though it had plenty, but for the stories it held. The hush of a bride's footsteps as she stepped inside, the breathless gleam in a groom's eyes as he caught his first glimpse, the trembling hands clasped together as vows were whispered like sacred secrets. It was the kind of place that didn't need a show, didn't beg for attention. It simply was.

And maybe that's why it tugged at me now. In the swirl of my own engagement, so full of glittering posts and photo-perfect smiles, I couldn't help but think of that chapel and its simple, steady truth. I had never been the girl to dream of lace trains or cascading bouquets, but if I had ever allowed myself to dream of a wedding, it would have been somewhere like that old chapel. Quiet, real, rooted. Not a performance, not a spectacle, just a promise, made honestly, under the trees where love had always bloomed.

But the wedding chapel I was facing, beautiful though it was, bathed in soft light and dressed for celebration, felt cold and stale, like a stage left empty too long after the curtain had fallen. Its walls seemed to resound with something empty. It did not offer the peace, the hope, the love I longed for. Instead, it carried a chill that settled in my stomach like a stone.

Each time I let my mind wander to that place, a slow pang twisted inside me. I would close my eyes and see it. There I was, dressed in white, walking the long aisle alone, the sound of my own footsteps louder than the music. Daniel waited at the altar, his dark eyes fixed forward, his practiced smile stretched thin, rehearsed for photographs more than for me. His family would fill the pews to my right, a sea of familiar faces polished to perfection, every smile wide, every posture pristine, all of them performing their part.

And on my side, only my grandma, her hands folded in her lap, her shoulders slightly bent with time, and my dad's brother with his quiet family beside him. Sparse. Silent. Strangers in a spectacle that was supposed to be mine. Would they smile for me, out of duty, or would their eyes betray the same twisting unease I felt? Would they see the tremor in my hands, the way my breath caught not with joy but with dread? I could almost hear the whispering questions ripple through the air like a breeze. Is she happy? Or is she afraid?

It was a dark, cool Tuesday evening, the kind where autumn whispered against the windows and the scent of pizza filled Todd's living room. Our little friend group had gathered to eat and play games, and as we began, Stephanie suddenly giggled, her cheeks blooming as red as her hair. Todd, sitting close beside her, wore a small, knowing smile that stretched wider by the second.

Then came the moment that shifted the room. Stephanie lifted her hand, and there it was, a glinting diamond ring catching the lamplight. "We're getting married!" she squealed, her voice bubbling over with delight. Todd beamed, and the air seemed to erupt. Chairs scraped, hands clapped, and voices rose in a flurry of questions.

What struck me most wasn't anxiety for them, though they had barely been dating long enough for the seasons to change, but envy. A sharp, quiet spasm pressed against my chest. Their love felt real, effortless, unperformed. Mine, by contrast, felt like a play staged under heavy lights. Stephanie's ring was much smaller than mine, but it was real. Everything was real.

As the evening unfolded, they shared their story. How the

feelings had begun long before the first secret date, how their bond had quietly grown in the spaces none of us had noticed. They spoke of their plans, a wedding just one month after Daniel and I would marry. But theirs would be different, small, intimate, stripped of spectacle. Her cousin would officiate in the modest church where she was raised, and only a handful of family and the three of us would attend. Todd's father, absent since his childhood, would not be there. Just his mother and grandparents, gathered in quiet pride. Stephanie's family would fill the rest of the pews, their faces familiar, their presence warm. It would be a ceremony made of harmony and sincerity, no excess, no staged perfection.

And as I watched them, I saw something rare. A promise that wasn't draped in glitter but woven in truth. Todd, in his steady way, had already been helping Stephanie shoulder her debts. He had vowed, not in vows yet spoken, but in the way he held her hand, to protect her, to choose her, to weather every storm with her. In good times and bad, in sickness and health, in scarcity and abundance, and yes, until death parted them.

Jealous. I was jealous. That sharp, aching kind of jealousy that isn't born of malice, but of longing. I wanted that kind of love. When I first met Todd, I'd sometimes wondered if he had a crush on me, but now I understood. What I had felt was something else entirely. Todd had a brotherly affection, a quiet guardianship. That was just who he was, a real man, the kind who poured goodness into his friends without keeping score, who offered protection without pride, kindness without calculation.

And now, as I watched him with Stephanie, I saw what real devotion looked like. He loved her, truly loved her. Not the kind of love that reshapes someone into a mirror of your own desires, but the kind that lets them shine as they are. He laughed when she spoke her mind, unfiltered and fearless. He adored that boldness. His eyes softened whenever they met hers, lit with something deeper than infatuation. It was genuine, pure love.

And her? She looked at him as though he hung the stars. Older than him by three years, yet in his presence, she seemed lighter, younger, as though he made her soul skip. She admired him. She respected him. She trusted him. How had we missed this quiet blooming all these months? It was right there, hidden in plain sight, a picture of profound love revealed in the simplest, most ordinary gestures.

And I, sitting just a few feet away with a heavy fake ring on my finger and a heavier heart, was jealous. But I was happy, too. Happy for them, and maybe even more aware of what was missing in me. I hugged them both. A tiny tear escaped and slid down my cheek as I whispered in Stephanie's ear, "I'm so happy for you."

Daniel offered his congratulations, all smiles and polished charm, saying every word one would expect, at exactly the right time. But his eyes never stayed too long on them, never softened in that way people's eyes do when they feel a story deeply. He was wrapped up in his own world, his plans, his image, and though he suggested we pop open champagne, I knew he didn't care about the beauty of their bond.

Then there was Jackie. Her silence carried enormous weight. Her jealousy was not like mine. It didn't just twist with envy for what they had. It hollowed her out with what she didn't. There she sat, the lone single among our group of five, not engaged, not claimed, and somehow marked by that absence as though it were a flaw. I watched her offer hugs and smiles that didn't quite reach her eyes. She whispered her best wishes, her voice a little too light, a little too bright, the kind of tone one wears like a mask. And underneath that mask, I saw her pain. So pretty. So polished. So endlessly alone. It felt unfair, the way love had passed her heart by. I wished I could take her hand, slip her out of that room, and let her cry without shame. Oh, Jackie. My dear, sweet Jackie. The loneliness was a shadow wrapped around her shoulders, too heavy for her delicate frame.

Time was ticking away, and the wedding was getting closer. Somewhere deep in my chest, beneath the noise of planning and pretending, a whisper told me I needed one more moment, one more breath of that place where my soul felt whole. So I packed a bag, claimed a long weekend, and left the city behind. I traded its sirens and streetlights for the winding roads that led home, where the air smelled of fallen leaves and cool earth, where the wind carried the soft hush of trees instead of the hum of traffic. There, the nights came alive with my stars, real stars, countless and unpolluted, strewn across the midnight sky like the universe had poured out its jewelry box.

Grandma was waiting, frailer than the last time I'd seen her, yet still sharp in spirit. We spent the evenings curled up in her living room, sipping tea under cozy blankets, our voices low as the clock ticked. We talked about everything, about life, about love, about what lasts when the glitter fades.

When she finally drifted to sleep, I would slip out into the night and tilt my head back toward that endless black velvet dome. I searched for their faces there. Mom, Dad, Simon, my constellation of family. I could almost see Dad's proud smile, Mom's gentle eyes, and Simon's mischievous wink. It was as if the stars themselves pulsed with their love, sending it down in silvery threads to weave around my aching heart. The magic of those nights filled me up in a way nothing else had for months. Beneath those stars, I felt not lost, but found.

On my last day there, we went to church. Grandma led us to her usual spot, the very front row, close enough to catch every word, every hymn. The service passed in a warm, familiar haze, and when the final hymn rippled through the room, we rose to leave. And there he was.

Young. Rugged. Tall. The kind of presence that made the air feel a little thicker, the edges of the world a little sharper. He smiled as he bent down to hug Grandma, and that smile, oh, that smile, stopped me. It was wide and genuine, full of the kind of goodness you can't fake. For a moment, my chest fluttered because it reminded me of my dad, open, kind, steady. His eyes were deep green, the color of pine forests after rain, and his hair was light brown, thick, tousled, a little wild. Grandma chatted with him briefly, then turned with a soft beam in her eyes. "My dear, I'd like you to meet my granddaughter, Callie."

He turned toward me, offered his hand, and when our fingers met, my heart beat like it had been startled awake. "Callie," Grandma said, "this is Caleb. He bought the ranch." Our words, polite and simple, didn't match the electricity that ran beneath them. "Nice to meet you." Nice to meet you, too." But inside, I shook. Caleb had the warmth of Mom's light, the quiet strength of Dad's steady hands, and, somehow, the easy charm of Simon's grin. It was as though the three of them had conspired in heaven to send me this stranger wrapped in their best pieces, standing there with a presence that felt both new and strongly familiar.

Soon, he was gone, vanishing into the after-church crowd with a polite nod and that unforgettable smile. We stepped out into the cool air to head back to Grandma's apartment, where I packed my things slowly. My heart craved that town, clinging to the scent of autumn leaves and Grandma's gentle presence. I wished I could stay. I wanted to drive out to the ranch, to see the porch bathed in the late-afternoon sun, to find Caleb leaning against the rail, hands in his pockets, waiting. I wanted to hear the creak of the barn doors, the whisper of the fields. I wanted to never leave. But I did.

With a lump in my throat, I hugged Grandma goodbye, her arms fragile but full of the kind of strength you only recognize when you're about to lose it, and I drove away. Away from the quiet. Away from the stars that had always been mine. Back to the noise, the fumes, the restless city streets that did not feel like home. Back to a looming wedding that now felt like a sentence rather than a celebration. Back to a life I had built in haste, one that fit like someone else's dress, tight, awkward, unforgiving.

On the road, my thoughts betrayed me. They circled back to Caleb. I knew almost nothing about him, just whispers from Grandma months ago. A young cowboy who had bought the ranch, who reminded her of my dad. Had she mentioned he was single? I couldn't remember. I hadn't seen a ring. He hadn't greeted us with a woman at his side. And when I caught myself daydreaming about his voice, his hands, his smile, I gripped the wheel tighter and snapped myself out of it. "You're getting married, Callie," I muttered, the words like a cold splash of icy water.

When I walked into my apartment, the quiet felt heavy. I vaguely remembered that Daniel and I were supposed to have dinner with his parents that evening, a thought that made my stomach burn. I almost texted him to say I was home, to ask what time I should be ready, when my phone buzzed. A message from Daniel. "Don't worry about dinner tonight. I'm sure you're tired. Jackie came with me. I'll call tomorrow."

I stared at the screen. For a second, I couldn't even process it. Jackie? Jackie went with him? As much as I had dreaded that dinner, and as much as I was beginning to dread the wedding itself, the idea that he thought it was acceptable to take her to his parents' house burned through me like a match to dry grass. And Jackie. What made her think that was okay? My mind spun, dragging up recent memories like thorns. That road trip to the lake house, the two of them sipping wine at 2:00 in the morning, their quiet laughter. My blood boiled.

I wasn't one to get angry much. Of course, everyone gets angry sometimes, and I was no exception. But I'd never felt like this. This was a rage that made my fingers twitch and my throat ache to scream. Instead, I said nothing. I didn't reply. I dropped my phone on the bed and sat down beside it, my chest rising and falling too fast.

The binder of wedding receipts lay on the floor, a fat, accusing thing. I picked it up, flipped it open. The wedding chapel stared back at me, those glossy photos, that empty promise of a perfect day. So pretty, and yet so vain. Without thinking, I ripped the photos out, shredded them in my hands, and let the pieces fall to the floor like autumn leaves. Then I crawled under my cozy blanket, the familiar comfort pulling me down, and as I drifted to sleep, my anger faded into something more dangerous. A longing. I thought of Caleb, his green eyes, his quiet strength. And for the first time in weeks, my breath slowed.

CHAPTER 19
Cold Winter's Chill

With only two weeks til the big day, Daniel and I sat in my apartment going over some of my mounting wedding bills. One that caught my eye was for the limo that would whisk us away after the final dance at the reception. It was the most expensive limo on the list, and Daniel and his mom had chosen it without me. Daniel was giddy as we poured through it all. But as a final payment for the wedding venue slipped onto the floor, I suddenly found my courage. It was as if the girl I had always been, quiet, steady, raised beneath wide skies on a simple ranch, rose from beneath the suffocating layers of grief, loss, and pretense. She whispered to me, urging me to remember who I was, to speak. My pulse thundered in my ears as I finally found the courage. I set the bill down, looked directly at him, and asked, my voice like a cold wind through an open window, "Why did you take Jackie to dinner last weekend?"

The words froze the room. For the first time, I saw

something break across Daniel's carefully composed face. Raw emotion flickered there. Guilt, sharp and unmistakable. It was the look of a man who had been caught, and for once, he didn't mask it with charm or confusion. He didn't fumble for excuses or turn my question into an insult about my insecurities. Instead, he said quietly, almost flatly, "I knew you would be upset by that." It wasn't an apology. It wasn't remorse. It was a confession without regret, the kind of admission given not because he felt sorry, but because he couldn't deny it any longer. And in that moment, my heart understood something my mind had been refusing to see. I was about to marry a man who wasn't afraid of betraying me. He was perhaps only afraid of being discovered.

Over the next four hours, it all came pouring out. Words and confessions tumbled into the air of my apartment until it felt like we were drowning in them, both gasping for breath. Every wall I had carefully built, every illusion cracked wide open.

I asked him about my ring. I asked him to tell me the truth, explain why he had purchased a fake one. His eyes darted away before he nodded. "I couldn't afford a diamond that size," he admitted, "but I wanted you to have one." For me? Or for his image? The question echoed in my head like a bell. I told him I didn't care about jewelry. I cared about honesty. My voice shook with the weight of it.

Then I brought up Jackie, how it had made me feel to find them side by side on the couch at the lake house, wineglasses in hand, their laughter too intimate, too close. How inappropriate it was to take her to dinner at his parents' house, as though she were the one he wanted to impress. I expected him to argue, to twist the story until I was the paranoid one. But this time, Daniel didn't fight. He confessed.

He told me that long before he and I met, he had fantasized about Jackie. That her beauty was intoxicating. That she was dazzling, unreachable, "out of his league." The air left my lungs. If Jackie had been too good for him, what did that make me? Had I been the consolation prize, the attainable one?

And then his voice turned cold, almost calculated. He told me he liked that I had no family. That it meant I would be folded into his family, molded into his life, reshaped until I fit the picture he wanted. He admitted he had seen me as someone he could control, someone vulnerable enough to anchor himself to. I was perfect, he said, because I was alone. My skin prickled with horror, yet he wasn't finished. He confessed that when he took Jackie home after dinner, their hug had held just a heartbeat too long, that their cheeks had brushed, that his lips had grazed her face so close to her mouth it had left him reeling. He said it with the casualness of a man describing a dream, not the devastation of a man who had betrayed the woman he claimed to love. I sat there in the ruins of our engagement, staring at a man I never really knew and never really loved. His truths felt like poison spilling across my apartment floor, and I couldn't tell which was worse, the lies he had lived, or the fact that he spoke the truth now without the slightest flicker of remorse.

And what about me? What did I need to confess? That I loved his honey-sweet kisses and the comfort of his arms, the illusion of belonging? That I had clung to him, and to

Todd, Stephanie, and Jackie, like makeshift replacements for the family I had lost? I did not love him. Not truly. What I loved was the idea of not being alone, the fragile scaffolding of connection that he provided. So I confessed. I told him I had played a role in this charade we called a relationship. I told him I didn't love him and didn't want to be bound to his tight-knit, controlling family. For once, the words flowed freely, without fear, without hesitation.

And so, we sat in that small apartment for hours, both of us pouring out the truths we had swallowed for too long. It was raw and messy, like vomiting out poison until there was nothing left. By the time our words ran dry, we were emptied and completely exhausted. We sat together on the floor, holding hands, not like lovers, not even like friends, but like two people who had just survived a wreck, clinging to one another in the aftermath. There was no romance in the gesture, only a shared acknowledgment of pain and failure.

A few minutes later, I released his hand. Quietly, deliberately, I slipped the engagement ring from my finger. Its weight felt foreign now, dishonest. I placed it in his palm, closing his fingers gently around it, sealing away everything it had once promised. The air around us, once sharp with confrontation, grew stale and heavy. We were calm. We knew what needed to be done. Tomorrow, there would be calls to make, deposits to forfeit, invitations to cancel. A wedding only two weeks away would have to be unraveled thread by thread. But that would come later. For now, there was only silence. For now, there was only us, sitting side by side in the wreckage, saying our goodbyes in the simplest way we knew how, not with anger, not with passion, but with the strange tenderness of two people finally telling the truth.

It wasn't winter, but the next day the wind cut like knives, carrying with it the brutally cold truth we now had to share with the world. I woke with the weight of it pressing on my chest. My first call was to Grandma. Her voice was sweet as sugar, warm as ever, but beneath it, I caught a piece of something else. Relief. She didn't say it outright, but I could hear it in her tone. She had never been truly comfortable with me marrying Daniel, and now I realized she had carried that quiet unease the whole time. I longed to be with her, to sink into her arms, to let her voice patch the jagged holes inside me. But there were more calls to make.

Jackie was next on my list. Jackie. The name alone made my stomach twist. How do you call the person who betrayed you? How do you form words for someone who faked happiness for you when really they were falling for your fiancé? I couldn't. Not yet. So I dialed Katie. It was an early Sunday morning, and I knew she'd been out late with Christian, but she answered anyway, her voice groggy but soft.

"Oh, Chica," she said softly, "I'm coming over with coffee."

Before I could protest, before I could even tell her not to, she hung up. And I knew better than to try again. Katie was already on her way, probably still in pajamas, arms full of Venti coffees and a box of donuts. She was that kind of friend.

While I tried to piece together what I could possibly say to Jackie, my phone buzzed. A text. It was her. "I heard. I'm coming over." Panic surged through me. The last thing I wanted was to face her while Katie was there. I didn't want my betrayal laid bare in front of someone else, no matter how loyal.

My fingers flew across the screen, "Please, wait. Give me an hour and I'll call you." Almost instantly, her reply flashed back. A heart emoji. Followed by a broken heart. And I sat there, staring at the glowing screen, wondering which one of those Jackie truly meant.

Katie flew straight into the role of comforting sister and, if such a thing existed, wedding de-coordinator. She plopped down on the floor with my big binder, the one Annette and her daughters had meticulously compiled, and began flipping through the tabs like a woman on a mission. Where Annette had seen order and perfection, Katie saw contracts and cancellation policies.

With only two weeks until the big day, I wouldn't see a cent of the deposits again, but thankfully, several of the final balances could be stopped before they drained more from me. I wasn't panicked about the money. Annoyed, yes, but mostly just grateful Katie was there to help untangle the mess. Most of the calls would have to wait until offices opened on Monday, but she managed to fire off several emails right away. I couldn't help but seethe at the irony. Annette had arranged nearly all the vendors, yet here I was, the one left to cancel everything and eat the cost. Another reminder of how little the wedding had actually been mine.

Katie scribbled down phone numbers in neat rows, building her to-call list for the morning. Then she paused, looking at me with soft eyes. "What about the dress? Do you want me to take it away?" The words hit harder than I expected. That stupid dress. Gorgeous, yes. Breathtaking, even. But not me. Not really. It was their version of a bride stitched into satin. I walked to the closet, pulled it out carefully, and let my fingers trail over the fabric. For a moment, I just stared at it, remembering the applause, the champagne, the cameras flashing as though I had stepped into someone else's fairytale. Then I turned, placed it in Katie's arms, and said simply, "Find somewhere to donate it." Done.

While Katie busied herself with notes and lists, my phone buzzed and lit up again and again. I didn't even glance at it. I knew Stephanie and Todd were probably calling. I knew Jackie's texts would keep coming, each one more insistent than the last now that an hour had passed. But I let the phone sit there, facedown, silent. For now, the only thing that mattered was Katie, steady, practical, unshaken. Her hands moved quickly over the pages, dismantling a wedding that had never truly belonged to me. And with every contract she crossed off, every vendor she prepared to call, I felt the tiniest bit lighter, as though with her help I could start peeling my life back into something that was my own again.

When Katie finally left, I was swallowed by the silence of my apartment. The kind of heavy silence that pressed in from all sides. Just over a year ago, I had walked through these very rooms with so much hope. My dad had been by my side that day, smiling with quiet pride, relieved that we had found a safe place in the city. I could still see him leaning against the doorframe, his eyes warm, his presence steady. The memory cracked something inside me. Suddenly, the tears came. Violent, unstoppable. Not delicate tears, but a flood. I wept, body shaking, as though torment had been dammed up and was now crashing through every fragile barrier I had built.

Everything about the past fourteen months spun through my mind like a storm I hadn't realized I was caught in. The roller coaster of the unimaginable loss of my dad, the dizzying pull of grief, the sudden embrace of new friends who felt like family, the whirlwind romance that had promised safety but delivered betrayal. I had been spinning so fast I hadn't been able to think, to breathe, to see where I was going.

Now the ride had stopped, and I was left dizzy, weeping. I wasn't crying for Daniel. My tears were for something much deeper, much older. They were for my parents. For my brother. For the town that had shaped me. For the girl I used to be, the one who had gotten buried beneath all the noise and chaos. I felt like I was standing outside in a black, howling storm, the cold wind tearing through me, leaving me small and alone and lost. My knees buckled beneath the weight of it, and I fell to the floor, my hands clutching at the carpet like it might hold me steady. "Dear God, please help," I sobbed, the words torn straight from my soul, ragged and desperate. That was all I could manage. A prayer stripped bare, but it was the truest one I had ever spoken.

When I finally gathered the strength to stand, I reached for my phone. The screen lit up with a flood of missed calls and texts. Uncle Jeremy had left a voicemail, his voice steady, tender, promising love from him and Aunt Kathy and asking me to call when I felt ready. If I couldn't have my dad at that moment, I'm glad I could have his brother.

The rest of the notifications blurred together. Message after message from Stephanie, Todd, and Jackie. But what struck me most wasn't what I saw. It was what I didn't see. Nothing from Daniel. Not a single word. Not a text, not a missed call. Just silence. I wasn't sure why I expected something from him. What more could possibly be said after last night? And yet, some small, aching part of me had still hoped for a scrap of recognition. Even Annette and Bob, or one of the sisters, at least Jenna, might have reached out. But there was nothing. Silence from the Masters family was louder than any storm, and in that silence, I felt the full weight of just how disposable I must have been to them.

Before calling Jackie, I closed my eyes and prayed. My words were clumsy but heartfelt, "Lord, help me be kind. Help me be patient. Help me listen without judgment." When Jackie finally answered, I could hear the strain in her voice. Her words came out shaky, edged with nerves, and I couldn't tell if she had been crying or was just frightened of what this conversation might bring.

"Are you okay?" she asked quickly, almost as though she had to get it out before I could say anything else. Our conversation was brief, but one thing she told me lodged like a thorn under my skin. Daniel had called her early that morning to tell her that I had broken off the engagement.

Confusion twisted in my chest. Wasn't last night mutual? We had both spoken the truth, both admitted our failures, both sat in that wreckage together. Yes, I had slipped the ring into his hand first, but hadn't it been clear to us both that it was the only possible ending? But now, another thought began to creep in, dark and unsettling. Was Daniel already shaping the story to his advantage? Was he going to cast me as the one who ended things, painting himself as the victim? It wasn't far-fetched. He had, after all, been engaged before. The tale I'd been told was neat and easy, that she was "crazy," that she had "dumped him" to marry his friend. But standing there now, phone pressed to my ear with Jackie's shaky voice on the line, I felt the ground tilt beneath me. Had that really been the truth? Or was I just the next chapter in a story Daniel had been writing all along?

Jackie and Stephanie both arrived at my apartment in the early evening, pizza and sodas in hand. We sat on the floor without saying much. It was Stephanie who finally spoke. "Why did you break up with him, Callie?"

The question hit me like ice water. Her words sounded strange, twisted. My confusion must have shown on my face, because she hurried on. "I mean, Daniel called us this morning, really early. He was crying. He said you just, out of nowhere, changed your mind about everything. That you pulled off the ring and threw it at him."

I blinked at her, my pulse drumming in my ears. "He said what?"

Jackie nodded reluctantly, her eyes looking down at her slice of pizza as though it held answers she couldn't say out loud. "He told me the same thing," she whispered. "That he didn't even see it coming, that you blindsided him."

The room tilted. This wasn't just Daniel reshaping the truth to soften his pride. This was a full, deliberate lie. Not a shaded version of events, not an omission. A complete rewrite of the night we had shared, the four hours of confessions, the ring placed gently in his hand. A hot, angry flush spread across my chest. For a moment, I couldn't find my voice. All I could think was, of course. Of course, Daniel would want the world to see him as the poor, abandoned one. It explained why I hadn't heard from him or his family. He had already cast me as the villain in their story.

Somehow, I managed to choke out the words, "It was mutual." But even as I said it, I knew how little those words mattered now. Whoever gets to everyone first is the winner in these battles, and Daniel had beaten me to it by miles. He'd called them all in the dead of morning, spinning his story while I was still trying to breathe through the wreckage.

Daniel had an image to uphold. His whole family did. With a wedding only two weeks away, two hundred invitations sent, gowns and suits pressed, gifts stacked neatly in their living room, there had to be an explanation. Not a true one, of course, but a polished one. And the only story that covered their humiliation was the one that painted me as cruel. Heartless Callie, who coldly tossed aside their golden boy.

I could already imagine it. Friends gathering at the Masters' house, sympathy dripping like honey as they rallied around the "betrayed" fiancé. Bottles of wine offered, casseroles delivered, voices lowered into gossipy tones about how I had deceived Daniel into thinking I was a sweet, simple country girl. Annette and Amanda plotting over the phone, piecing together the narrative like publicists in damage control. Bob, shaking his head with solemn dignity, pretending to be the noble father protecting his son's broken heart. And Leslie, grinning that sharp little grin of hers, the one that always carried a hint of satisfaction in other people's misery. Would

Jenna join them, too? Sweet Jenna, who sometimes seemed apart from their schemes. Or would even she be pulled into the "Poor Daniel" chorus, her voice blending with the rest in the Callie-bashing symphony I knew was already underway?

To my surprise, the next several weeks passed with me completely tossed aside by them all. Daniel. His family. Jackie. Stephanie. Even Todd. Todd, of all people, the one I had truly believed was a loyal and steadfast friend, never once called to ask what had really happened. He was engaged to Stephanie, so maybe it made sense that he chose her side to believe that I had dumped a man two weeks before our wedding. The silence from Todd cut deeper than I expected. I had trusted him, counted on him, and he was gone, just like the rest. Somehow, they all just believed I was cruel, and they left me.

It stunned me, the speed of their abandonment. One moment, they had swept into my life like a rescue team, pulling me out of the darkness of grief and loss, offering laughter and dinners and companionship. The next moment, they vanished, leaving me stranded in the very same darkness, only this time it felt colder, lonelier, more treacherous than before.

Winter came with a vengeance, as if the weather itself mirrored my inner world. Brutal winds rattled my windows, snow piled on the streets, and ice glazed the sidewalks until the city seemed encased in glass. Katie tried. She showed up with her sunshine personality and her constant plans, pulling me out for coffee or insisting I join her on errands just so I wouldn't stay cooped up. But soon she was swept up in her own whirlwind. Her summer wedding to plan, her excitement for the future. And I couldn't expect her to shoulder my broken pieces while building her own joy.

So I learned to live in the silence. To sit alone at night with the lights turned off, staring out my window at the glittering city skyline that felt more like a taunt than a comfort. To sink into the same reruns of Gilmore Girls until the voices of fictional people became my only company. To go to bed early, wake up, go to work, and repeat the cycle with machine-like regularity. At the office, I kept my head down. Paul stopped by once, offered his condolences, but even that rang hollow. I could tell he had never thought I belonged with Daniel in the first place.

Church became impossible. I couldn't stomach walking in and seeing all of them, their hugs, their warmth, their community that had once included me. I stayed away, though sometimes, late at night, I'd sneak onto social media to peek at their lives. Was Daniel with Jackie now? Were Todd and Stephanie already married? Did they talk about me at all, or was I already erased from their memories, replaced by new stories and new people?

The weeks dragged on, and little by little, I began to feel myself dissolve. I wasn't Callie anymore. Not the girl who used to laugh, or love, or dream. I was only the outline of her. A shell. An empty shell, lost in a cold winter's chill on my way to freezing to death.

Crews

CHAPTER 20
Field of Wildflowers

When I was five years old, my mom and I spent an afternoon out in the sunshine picking flowers. Every spring, one of our fields would explode into color, a sea of blossoms stretching as far as my little eyes could see. Wildflowers weren't common where we lived. Neighbors might have a handful scattered here and there, but somehow, we had an entire field overflowing with them, swaying like waves in the breeze. I remember that day so vividly. The sky impossibly blue, the air sweet, and my mom twirling barefoot among the blossoms as if she had been waiting her whole life to dance in that moment.

I trailed after her, clutching a fistful of daisies, and asked in my small, curious voice, "Mom, why do we have so many flowers just in this one big field?" She laughed softly, kneeling down so her hazel eyes were level with mine, and she told me one of the most precious stories I've ever carried in my heart.

Back in high school, when she was dating my dad, he once surprised her with a bouquet of roses. Pink roses. Lovely, carefully arranged, wrapped in paper, and tied with a bow. She had thanked him with a smile, but he could see something was missing in her expression, a spark that wasn't quite there. So he asked her gently if she didn't like roses. And my mom, in her loving, graceful way, told him she absolutely appreciated the gift, but confessed that the manicured, florist's roses weren't her favorite. What she loved most were flowers that grew wild, free, untrimmed, kissed by sun and wind. She dreamed, she said sweetly, of someday dancing in a wide open field filled with them.

Years later, when they were newly married and had just bought their first little piece of land, my dad remembered. Without telling her, he went out with bags of wildflower seeds and scattered them over an empty field. He kept his secret through the winter, and then, come spring, the earth came alive. Reds and yellows, blues and purples, thousands of blooms nodding in the breeze. One afternoon, he led her out there with a picnic basket and her favorite tunes, and when she saw what he had done, she burst into squeals of joy. Then he took her hand and they danced together in the middle of that wildflower field until the sun dipped low.

Even at five years old, I knew that was the most romantic story I would ever hear. And even now, it holds onto me like perfume, a reminder that love, real love, doesn't need spectacle or performance. It just needs to plant itself deep and grow wild.

As the bitter cold of winter finally loosened its grip, I managed to crawl into the beginnings of spring. The season didn't bring joy, not exactly, but it carried a faint whisper of relief. I had thrown myself into work with a kind of ruthless determination, and it paid off with a promotion I hadn't even seen coming. My evenings, once filled with silence and shadows, now often included helping Katie plan the little details of her wedding at the end of June. I wasn't happy, not the kind of happy that lights up the soul, but I was no longer drowning either. Just floating. Surviving.

Still, social media had a way of reminding me how much had changed. That's where I learned that Stephanie and Todd had gotten married. Just a handful of photos, smiles from a small wedding. Missing were Daniel and Jackie. Jackie's social media accounts were all shut down. And Daniel? He had moved on.

There he was, arm in arm with Kendall Weaver, smiling in front of a massive Christmas tree in the lobby of his church. I knew the backdrop instantly. It was the very same spot where I once stood with him, waiting to be noticed. My stomach knotted when I realized the photo had clearly been taken months ago. While I was still piecing myself back together, he had already begun parading a new relationship. And Kendall. I remembered her vividly. The girl who rushed up to him that night after the Christmas Eve service, who embraced him with too much familiarity, who pulled his attention away while I stood invisible in the background. That was the moment I had felt abandoned, discarded in plain sight. Now there she was, the new prize, the next woman to be wrapped into the Masters' tight circle.

I felt a pang of sorrow for her. Not jealousy, not even anger, just sorrow. Did she know what it was to wear a fake ring, to smile for a performance while suffocating under the weight of expectations? Did she know how easily Daniel's family could make a cage look like a castle? I hoped she wouldn't find out. I hoped she would be spared.

But I couldn't stop thinking about my so-called friends, the ones I had clung to as though they were family. How easily they had dropped me, how quickly they had believed Daniel's version without once asking me what had really happened. My voice had never mattered. My perspective had never been wanted.

And then there was Jackie. Her absence haunted me more than the others. What was she doing now? Did she still see Daniel? Or had she been cast out, too? Were Todd and Stephanie still close with her, or had they drifted away once they settled into their marriage? For all her betrayal, I still cared about her. I couldn't help but wonder if Jackie was okay.

Then I went home. I packed a small bag for a week with Grandma and drove away, longing for peace. She looked so frail when I arrived, so tired from all the years of carrying grief. Loss had carved its lines into her face, but her eyes still carried a quiet light. We spent our days on the couch, side by side, paging through old photo albums, remembering the ones we loved, the ones who now belonged to the heavens. We cried until our voices broke, then laughed until our stomachs ached, the way only shared memory can weave sorrow and joy together.

In those moments, I realized just how much I adored her. I saw my dad in the twinkle of her eyes, heard his laugh in the warmth of her voice. Being near her felt like brushing up against the pieces of him I'd been missing. More than anything, I recognized how much I longed to be like her. To carry strength the way she did, not loud or boastful, but steady and unwavering.

Grandma lived with a sense of purpose that stretched beyond the here and now. For her, life was about eternity. Her calling was both simple and profound, to love people well, to shine God's love through her smiles and small gifts. In just a few short days, I felt something awaken inside me. I wanted that too. I didn't know how much longer I would have her, but I knew that whatever time we had left, I wanted to learn from her. To watch her, to soak up her wisdom, and to walk in the kind of grace she carried so effortlessly.

One morning, I woke with a fierce ache I couldn't ignore, a pull toward the ranch. It had been so long. Spring had come, and with it, my mom's wildflowers in her field. I longed to throw myself into their colors, to breathe in the sweetness of that place, to stand where my parents and Simon once stood and feel, if only for a moment, whole again.

The ranch wasn't mine anymore. It belonged to someone else now, Caleb. I hadn't dared to ask Grandma much about him. I didn't want to betray the truth of my restless heart, the way my mind had wandered to him in secret moments. I didn't even know if he was married or if there was someone waiting for him at night. It didn't matter. I wasn't going there for him. At least, that's what I told myself.

I needed the wildflowers. I needed the air. So, I asked Grandma if she thought it would be all right to visit. Her eyes lit up immediately, her smile warm as spring sunshine.

"We should both go," she said, already reaching for the phone. She called Caleb to let him know, and he said he'd be happy to have us.

The drive felt like shedding a heavy coat. With every mile of winding dirt road, the air grew fresher, the sky turned a deeper blue, and the sun hung bold and golden over the pastures. When I opened the gate, the memory of my dad struck me like a breeze. His boots in the dust, his hat tipped low, the familiar scent of hay and earth clinging to his embrace. I could almost see him, arms outstretched. Oh, Dad. I swallowed the lump in my throat.

We pulled into the drive, gravel crunching beneath the tires, and there he was. Caleb. He walked out with an easy confidence, a piece of straw between his lips, and tipped his hat in greeting. He hugged Grandma first, warm and genuine, then turned to me. His hand reached for mine, strong, calloused, steady. "Welcome home, Callie," he said, his voice low, his green eyes catching the sunlight.

Caleb stayed on the porch with Grandma while I wandered down the familiar path toward the wildflower field. The grass whispered under my feet, and the air held that sweet, earthy scent I had missed for far too long. Grandma told him about this place, how my dad planted those flowers years ago as a gift to my mom. Caleb hadn't known the story, but when she shared it, he smiled and said the field seemed to be waiting, alive and patient, blooming just for me.

When I saw the colors spread across the hillside, yellows like morning sun, purples deep as twilight, my breath caught. I ran the last few steps and fell to my knees, pressing my palms into the warm earth. The tears came fast, hot against the cool breeze. "Oh, Mom," I whispered, my voice swallowed by the open sky. I closed my eyes and saw her, barefoot in the field, laughing, twirling as the wind carried her hair like a ribbon. For a moment, I was a little girl again, watching her spin in the flowers she loved so much. I picked a handful, golden and violet, and slowly made my way back to the porch.

That porch. How many summer nights had I spent there, chasing fireflies with Simon, sipping lemonade with Dad, feeling safe, whole, home? Nothing had changed. Caleb had kept it all as it was. He stood when I approached, and smiled, his rugged cheeks glowing. "Here," he said, his voice low and steady, "you'll want this." In one hand, he held a chilled glass of lemonade for me. In the other, a mason jar filled with water for my flowers. We sat there together, talking about the simplest things. The stars that twinkled like diamonds over the pasture at night, the hush of mornings before the cattle stirred, the way the sunset painted the land gold before giving it back to the moon.

Caleb shared pieces of himself without trying to impress me. He was thirty. Unmarried. His family owned a farm about eighty miles away, and he had grown up in a town not unlike mine. He had studied to be a veterinarian but chose the life of a cattleman instead. As he spoke, I learned he and my dad had crossed paths many times at cattle auctions. My dad, he said, had been a mentor, someone who always had a word of advice or a steadying hand for a young man trying to find his way. And now here he was, living alone on this ranch that once held my childhood. He hadn't changed a thing. Not the porch, not the fences, not even the old windmill that creaked in the breeze. And now that he knew the story of the field, he looked at me and said quietly, almost like a promise, "I'll never change that. Not a single flower."

CHAPTER 21
The Road Home

At twenty-three, I learned that life rarely travels in a straight line. It bends, it twists, it lures you down roads you never expected to take. In college, I had longed for a new road, something bold, something that would shake loose the dust of the past and give me a clean slate. I thought the city would do that for me. Its bright lights promised movement, change, distraction. I thought I could leave the quiet fields behind and, with them, the sorrow I had carried since I was twelve.

But the truth was far more complicated. Different doesn't always mean better. The city, with all its noise and glitter, became a place where my grief did not fade. It multiplied. The anguish that once lived quietly in my chest grew heavier, more demanding, until it felt like a shadow I could never outrun. Loss met loss, piling high like stones I could not carry, and I began to realize that not every place is meant to hold your heart. There are places that accept you, cradle you, whisper you home, and there are places that drain you until you forget who you were meant to be.

My visit to our family's ranch didn't just stir a desire to return. It awakened a need so deep it felt like a heartbeat. I needed those wildflowers swaying in the wind. I needed the porch where the world slowed down and the stars came close enough to touch. I needed the winding roads that carried the scent of hay and rain and home.

It reminded me of *Gone With the Wind*, of Scarlett's final realization that her soul was tied to Tara, not because it was grand, but because it was her. The land had roots that reached into her heart, just as mine did into me. All the things I had chased, the glitter, the noise, the friends I thought were family, suddenly felt empty. I felt empty.

That day, I opened my eyes and saw what I had become, a stranger to my own heart. My soul was hurting not just for my mom, my dad, and my brother, but for the version of me I had left behind when I walked away from the place that raised me. I could not keep running. If I was ever going to find peace, I had to go back to the soil where my spirit once soared. But how? How was I supposed to find my way back?

Spring in the city was very rainy and windy that year. With little sunshine, I grew weak and depressed. Each day, the longing for home rooted itself deeper in me, twisting tighter, pulling harder. At first, it was just a quiet dream, a whisper in the back of my mind, "Go home." But a whisper became a plan. I polished my resume. My boss adored me. I knew she'd write a glowing reference the moment I said the word. That part would be easy.

But then came the questions. Where would I work? What

would I do? My hometown didn't have big accounting firms. There were no tall towers, no glass offices perched high above the streets. But that was the point. I was craving the simple life. I was craving peace. I could work at the bank. I could handle the books for the feed store. I could even start a small business, helping the people I grew up with manage their accounts and dreams. And truthfully, I didn't need to rush. My inheritance had given me the cushion to breathe, to figure things out. I imagined buying a little plot of land near the ranch, watching the seasons roll over the hills, living simply, quietly, happily.

A pang of regret pricked me then. I wished I hadn't sold the ranch. But as soon as the thought formed, so did another. Caleb. The name fluttered through me like a warm breeze. By then, I knew he was single, and that knowledge stirred something inside me, something I quickly scolded myself for. I could not go home for Caleb. That wasn't the reason, and it could never be. If I went home, it would be for me. For the girl I used to be. For the woman I still hoped to become. Even if I lived out the rest of my days alone, as long as I could breathe that country air and watch the stars over the fields near where my family once walked, I knew I would be at peace.

It was May, the kind of warm, blossoming May that felt full of promise, and Katie, in her usual way, was positively glowing. She radiated the kind of effortless joy that could pull anyone into its orbit. I found myself included in every moment of her wedding journey, from the first giggly brunches to the final fittings. I stood beside her as she picked her dress, just as she had been there when I picked mine. But

191

this time, the air felt different. Her smile was easy, unforced, her laughter genuine and light, a ribbon of happiness tying her and her mom together as they fussed over lace and satin.

The bridal shop seemed to revolve around her. Friends snapped photos, the staff couldn't help but watch nearby, and at one point, Katie, forever the life of the room, convinced the store manager to bring out a tray of sparkling tiaras for everyone to try on. We sipped champagne, a sea of glittering crowns perched atop our heads, and the flash of a camera caught us all mid-laugh, mid-toast. It was one of those photos that held the bright hum of celebration.

Katie made sure I was there for everything, every shower, every little surprise party, every toast and tasting. And through it all, she never stopped checking in with me. "Is this too much?" she would ask, her eyes soft, her voice laced with genuine care. She didn't want to rub salt in my wounds or make me feel like a shadow standing beside her spotlight. I cherished her for that.

And perhaps, in those weeks of glitter and giggles, I began to see the truth more clearly. Katie had been my only true friend in that city. Jackie, with her subtle little nudges, always urging me to try harder to fit into Daniel's world. Stephanie, with her quiet resentments, always looking at my financial circumstances as something to measure herself against. Todd, dear, confusing Todd, whose friendship I had trusted only to watch it dissolve into something cold and distant. And Daniel. Daniel hadn't truly seen me at all. He wanted to rewrite me, to sculpt me into some flawless reflection of the Masters family ideal.

But Katie never asked me to change. She liked me as I was.

She accepted me, even celebrated me, and that kind of friendship was rare. As I stood in that sparkling shop, tiara slipping in my hair and champagne glass warming in my hand, I knew that even as my time in that city drew to a close, hers was a friendship I would carry with me always.

In June, I finally turned in my two weeks' notice, a small act with enormous weight. Grandma had already been busy weaving a path home for me. She had spoken to an old family friend, a man who had grown up alongside my dad and uncle, now the managing partner of a small law firm in town. At first, they were only looking for part-time accounting help, someone to keep the books tidy and the office humming. But when he heard I was coming home, we had a phone interview, or rather, a warm conversation sprinkled with memories of my dad. By the end of the call, he offered me full-time employment with benefits. I'd handle both accounting and office management, working alongside three partners who served the people I'd grown up with, the farmers, the shopkeepers, the families who'd been part of our town's fabric for generations. It wasn't a grand office with marble floors or skyline views. It was a handful of cozy rooms in a weathered building on the town square, its front windows catching the golden light of late afternoons. Next door was Miss Sarah's Home Cooking, a restaurant that smelled of buttered biscuits and strong coffee, the kind of place where breakfast plates were big and gossip was free. I would start at the end of the month, just after Katie's wedding. It felt right. One chapter closing, another quietly opening.

Ahead of the move, I drove into town to start the hunt for

a place to live. I didn't expect anything more than a few viewings and a quiet lunch, but life has its way of surprising you. As I stepped out of my car in the grocery store parking lot, I caught sight of a familiar figure across the rows of trucks and cars. Tracie. My Tracie. My best friend from home, the girl I'd shared secrets and sleepovers and a thousand after-school milkshakes with.

We ran to each other like no time had passed, our arms locking tight, our laughter catching the attention of passersby. Tracie had left right after graduation, chasing her future to a faraway college and later to her family's beach house, where she'd built a life surrounded by salty air and seagulls. I had assumed that's where she'd always stay. But here she was, back in our little town, her eyes softer now, her smile both familiar and tinged with worry.

Her mother had been diagnosed with cancer and would be traveling for treatments in a hospital several hours away. Tracie had come home to care for the house and to be close, just in case. There was sadness in her voice, but also a thread of hope, hope that the treatment would work, that her mother's strength would carry them through. She had already taken a job teaching at the middle school, the very halls we'd once roamed with scraped knees and oversized backpacks.

We stood in that parking lot for what felt like forever, swapping memories of homecoming dances, bonfires, and all the small-town mischief we'd once sworn we'd never tell. The circumstances weren't happy, not entirely, but the reunion was. For the first time in a long time, I felt the warmth of a homecoming beginning to take shape, not just in the land or the job waiting for me, but in the people who were finding their way back, too.

I drew in a deep, steady breath, filling my lungs with the air I had hoped for, dusty dirt roads laced with the scent of hay, the faint musk of cattle carried on a warm breeze, the unmistakable sweetness of small-town goodness. It wrapped around me like a memory and a promise all at once. For the first time in what felt like forever, I was on the right road, the road that led me home.

Crews

CHAPTER 22
Caleb

Katie's wedding was nothing short of magical, a celebration drenched in love, laughter, and the kind of dancing that makes the floorboards sing. Christian was her perfect match, the calm to her sparkle, the strength to her fire. The way he looked at her, like she was the only woman in the world, made my heart burst. And Katie? She gazed at him as though he were the greatest man to ever walk the earth. Together, they radiated something rare, joy so vibrant it wrapped around everyone in the room. They hugged, they kissed, they pulled people into their world and made them feel like part of their happiness.

I sat with my coworkers, including Paul and his date, Rachel. At one point, while nearly everyone else had taken to the dance floor, Paul leaned in and started talking about Daniel and the others from my old circle of friends. It wasn't gossip, at least it didn't feel like that. It was more like an update from another lifetime.

197

Daniel was engaged to Kendall. Paul said she was just like Annette, which somehow made sense. He'd always been intensely bound to his mom. Todd and Stephanie had moved to another state where Todd had landed a high-paying job he couldn't turn down. Stephanie was pregnant, and they were doing well. Jackie was the mystery. She'd vanished, Paul said, stopped going to church after my breakup with Daniel, and no one seemed to know where she'd gone. A pang of sadness pressed into me. Jackie had mattered once. Even with the bitterness of her crush on Daniel, I cared about her, and the thought of her drifting away into silence saddened me.

But that world wasn't mine anymore. Katie's wedding was my curtain call, my final bow in the city. My bags were already packed, and my heart was finally ready to go home.

It was a picture-perfect June morning, the kind that hinted at fresh starts and second chances. The moving truck had already gone, carrying my belongings toward the place that had always quietly waited for me, home. I wasn't far behind, my SUV trailing the streets I once thought would lead me to a great new life. As the city skyline shrank in my rearview mirror, a deep, settling calm began to rise within me.

For the last time, I wove through those streets choked with traffic and noise, past towers of steel and glass that had never quite felt like mine. Each mile peeled away a layer of heaviness I hadn't realized I was still carrying. And then, the pavement loosened into the long, winding country roads that knew the song of my childhood. The air smelled sweeter. The sky seemed wider. Even the silence felt like an embrace.

I didn't know what waited for me on the other side of this

journey, what triumphs or trials, what surprises or scars. But I finally knew where my life would be lived, where my roots reached deepest. I knew where I belonged. My life had been shaped by pain as much as by joy. I had suffered losses that carved holes in my heart, losses that time could not erase. I understood now that grief is not something you get over, as people like to promise. It is something you carry, something that shifts shape as the years pass. It softens, perhaps, but it never disappears. It becomes part of you, like a scar that tells a story.

I would always miss them, Mom, Dad, Simon. I would always mourn what was taken. But I was ready to learn how to live with that sorrow, to let their memory be more than a weight. I wanted their memory to be a lantern, a source of quiet joy even as the anguish remained. And as the road stretched before me, lined with green grass and yellow flowers, shimmering in the early sun, I felt something I hadn't felt in a long time, peace. Not the loud, triumphant kind, but a tender, steadying peace that whispered, "You're going home."

My move into a small house on a two-acre plot was easy. The land stretched quietly, its edges brushing against my family's old ranch, and from the porch, I could almost trace the lines of my childhood across the fields. I told myself this was why I chose it, because I wanted to feel my family close again, to let the breeze carry whispers of their laughter across the grass. But deep down, beneath all the sensible reasons, there was a truth I dared not speak aloud. I hoped to see Caleb. I hoped for chance encounters at the fence line, for a smile across the field, for something gentle and new to take root.

It was then that I began to realize a hard truth. I had never truly been in love. I had been engaged to Daniel, yes, and there were moments I longed for his warm honey kisses, but I never truly longed for him. He was a patch over a wound, a temporary balm for the grief that had deflated me.

But Caleb was different. He was cut from the same cloth as the men I loved most. A cowboy, a rancher, quiet and steady, his strength as natural as the earth he walked on. And he was handsome. Those deep green eyes, those broad shoulders, those strong hands, those perfect lips I had imagined kissing. I wondered if what I felt was real or just the replica of a girlhood fantasy, the kind you paint on a young heart when you don't yet know what love is. Was this a crush? Or was it the first stirring of something true, something grown and lasting?

One week after my move, I picked up Grandma and drove her to church. As always, we settled into her favorite spot, the front pew, where she could see and hear every word. That morning, the message was about love shown through deeds, not just words. As I listened, my thoughts drifted to my parents and to Simon. That was exactly how they had lived. They didn't just say kind things. They acted them out in big and small ways. They were generous, never too busy to lend a hand, always willing to go the extra mile.

Sitting there, I felt a shift stir inside me. For the first time in a long time, something clicked. My move home wasn't just about starting over or hiding from pain. It was about stepping into something bigger. I was here to carry my family's legacy forward. To live with the same wide-open compassion as Mom, whose heart bent toward anyone who was hurting. To offer the same warmth and welcome as Simon, who had a gift for making everyone feel like they belonged. To honor Dad's deep love for the land and for the beauty of God's creation. In that moment, it hit me that I wasn't only here to heal. I was here with a purpose, to live like them, to love like them. A smile spread across my face as tears welled in my eyes. I could almost feel their arms wrap around me from above, their joy spilling into me, their spirits awakening in my own.

Grandma and I rose at the final "Amen," and began making our way toward the door. And then I saw him. My heart skipped a beat, then began pounding so fast I could hear it in my ears. A warm rush surged through me, tingling all the way down to my fingertips.

He was ahead of us, just stepping into the glow of the summer morning. From behind, I noticed the worn denim hugging his frame and the easy confidence in the way he walked. His tan cowboy boots clicked softly against the wooden floor, and as he pushed the door open, he slid a straw cowboy hat onto his head, the kind my dad used to wear when the days grew long and hot. Then he turned.

The sunlight caught his face, and I was suddenly rooted to the floor. His green eyes met mine, steady and unflinching, as if they'd been waiting for me all along. They pierced through me, straight into the quiet places of my soul I thought no one could see. A slow smile tugged at his lips, and his strong jaw looked almost too perfect, like something chiseled by the hand of God Himself.

"Hi, Mrs. Williams," he said warmly, nodding toward my

grandma with such respect that I saw her cheeks flush with pleasure. Then he turned back to me, and in one graceful motion, he tipped his hat, just like my dad used to do. "I'm so happy to see you, Callie," he said, his voice a smooth blend of warmth and strength. "Glad to know you've moved home."

I opened my mouth, but no words came. My throat was tight, my thoughts scattered. I was joy and nerves and something deeper, all swirling at once. Every part of me wanted to leap forward, to close the space between us, to press myself against him and taste those rugged lips. Instead, I just stood there, trembling, breathless, and entirely undone.

I was so grateful when Grandma made the first move. "Caleb, dear, would you care to join us for lunch?" Oh, Grandma, thank you! Caleb's eyes lit up, and much to my delight, he agreed without hesitation.

A few minutes later, the three of us were tucked into a corner booth at Miss Sarah's, the window beside us framing the small-town square like a picture. The summer sun spilled through the glass, shining a light upon us. Conversation came easily, as though we'd been waiting years to sit across from one another. I told Caleb about my new job that would begin the very next morning, right there next door to the restaurant. He leaned in, listening with his whole being, not just nodding politely, but watching me, asking thoughtful questions, and holding my gaze like every word I spoke mattered.

That was when it struck me. In all the months I'd spent with Daniel, he had never once been this interested in my world. He never asked about my work, or my family, or the little pieces of life that made me me. He grew restless when I mentioned my grief, impatient when I spoke of home. He had dismissed the wildflowers, ignored the beauty of the stars overhead, and brushed off the stories of ranch life with the same indifference he used on me. Daniel's world had no room for mine.

But Caleb, he leaned into it all, as if each detail were a thread he wanted to weave into his understanding of me. And I wanted to know about him, too. That day, I learned about his own hometown just eighty miles away. He painted a picture of it so vividly I could almost smell the hay and feel the arena dust. His little sister, Carrianne, was a barrel racer, fiery and fearless, he said with a grin that showed his pride. His younger brother, Cole, had once ridden broncs on the rodeo circuit but had traded that life for the steady flow of farming alongside their dad. His parents, high school sweethearts, had been married for nearly thirty-five years. The way Caleb spoke of them, his voice softened, his eyes brightened. I could hear the deep respect and affection threading through every word. They sounded so much like my own parents, steadfast, rooted, in love.

Grandma sat beside me, quiet but not silent. Her eyes twinkled with mischief, as though she were watching a story unfold that she'd already read the ending to. I could see she was growing tired, but there was no chance she'd cut the moment short. She let the conversation continue, let Caleb and me tumble deeper into the kind of talk that feels endless, like a stream running steady and clear.

In the weeks that followed, our moments together grew closer, longer, and sweeter. Neither of us dared to speak our feelings aloud, not yet, but we both knew. It was there in the way our eyes caught, in the pauses that neither of us rushed to fill, in the quiet pull of being near each other.

Caleb began sitting with Grandma and me on the front pew at church, his presence so steady and warm it almost felt as though he had been there all along. Afterwards, the three of us made it our tradition to go to lunch together, the kind of simple ritual that rooted itself in my heart.

During the week, when I came home from work tired and worn, Caleb would sometimes stop by. We'd sit in my living room with mugs of hot chocolate and talk for hours about nothing and about everything. Sometimes we laughed about the ordinary, silly details of life. Other times we wandered into the weightier things, loss, faith, dreams, and what it meant to truly belong somewhere. With him, the words came easily. He clung to mine as though they were treasures, and I clung to his, not out of desperation but because they nourished something deep inside me that had been starved for too long.

A bond was forming between us, not rushed or forced, but strong. Friendship first, then something far more tender. On weekends, he would invite me out to the ranch. He knew how much that porch meant to me, how I'd grown up on it, how my most precious memories of life were lived out on it. We would sit shoulder to shoulder, watching the sky turn to fire, then lavender, then deep indigo. When the stars began to appear, my heart always caught glimpses of my family's twinkling love. Caleb looked at me and smiled, not the kind of smile meant to charm, but the kind of smile that meant he understood. He let me talk about the stars, about the memories they carried of my parents and Simon. He didn't try to fix my grief or change the subject. He just listened, as though every memory was sacred. I knew then that he wasn't just looking at the stars with me. He was looking at them through me, past the night sky and into my heart.

And then, one early September evening, just before the stars began to pierce the fading blue sky, Caleb reached for my hand. His touch was steady, reverent, as though he knew he was holding something fragile yet sacred. Slowly, he lifted my hand to his lips. The kiss he placed there was soft but sure, a kiss that carried more weight than words ever could. Shivers rippled through me, not of cold but of awakening, as though every nerve in my body had suddenly remembered what it was meant to feel.

He drew me closer until I could feel the warmth of his chest pressed to mine, until I could hear the rhythm of his heartbeat answering the call of my own. His embrace wrapped around me, not only filling me with the heat of desire, but with something deeper, something that touched the marrow of my soul. It was as if he had reached beyond flesh and bone, straight into the essence of who I was, and held it tenderly in his arms.

We swayed there on the porch, without music, yet moved as though a melody only we could hear was guiding us. I breathed him in, the faint scent of cedar and hay, the warmth of late summer still clinging to his skin. I did not want to let go. Not ever. If I could have stopped time, I would have. In that sacred stillness, I knew. This was not infatuation, not illusion, not the desperate grasp for belonging I had once mistaken for love. This was real. This was steady. This was true. I loved him, fully, deeply, irrevocably. And I knew by the way his arms tightened around me, by the way his breath clung to my hair, that he loved me too.

CHAPTER 23
Beneath the Stars

Days later, Caleb invited me back to the porch. We had yet to go on what city people would call a "date," but that didn't matter. Lunches after church with Grandma, long talks in my living room, and these quiet evenings on the porch were far more meaningful than crowded restaurants or movie theaters.

The weather had shifted, summer heat giving way to the first whispers of autumn. A deep sapphire sky stretched endlessly over the ranch as hawks circled above us, their wings glowing gold in the last light of the day. We laughed, talked, and shared stories as if time didn't exist. Other than the gentle kiss he had placed on my hand days earlier, we had not yet crossed into anything more. But the air between us felt charged, alive, as though the earth itself was holding its breath, waiting.

As the sun sank low over the pasture, a chill crept into the breeze. Caleb disappeared for a moment, returning with a thick blanket. He wrapped it around my shoulders, his hands pausing there, warm and protective. Then his eyes met mine with a spark of mischief and tenderness all at once. "Let's go out to the pasture," he said. "Lay the blanket down and look at the stars."

Nothing in the world could have made me happier. A blanket under a sky full of stars, my favorite thing, my safe place, my dream. We carried the blanket out into the open pasture, spreading it on the cool ground before lying side by side. Darkness settled over us slowly, like a curtain lowering after a long day, and with every passing minute, more stars appeared until the heavens were spilling over with them. Brilliant, countless, endless, each one shining down as though they were witnesses to what was about to happen.

Caleb shifted closer, his arm brushing against mine, his warmth chasing away the chill. Without a word, his hand sought mine, strong fingers lacing perfectly with my own. Once more, he lifted my hand to his lips, his kiss gentle, a promise pressed against my skin. Then, with a trail of tenderness, he kissed my arm, my shoulder, my cheek. His big, steady arms wrapped around me, drawing me into his strength, and with every touch, I felt myself dissolving into him.

Finally, his lips found mine. Soft at first, questioning, like he was asking permission. His kiss tasted like warm vanilla, sweet and steady, familiar and yet completely new. My breath caught as his lips parted mine, and I melted against him. His hands framed my face with such care, fingers brushing my cheeks, cradling my ears, resting at the curve of my neck. His breath was warm against my skin, sending chills racing down my spine even as his embrace kept me steady. There, beneath the vast cathedral of stars, we didn't need words. Our kisses said everything. They were our vows, our confessions, our declarations of love. And though neither of us spoke the words aloud, I knew, we both knew, that this was love, pure and real, written beneath the stars.

As time marched on, our love only deepened. His family embraced me fully, as though I had always belonged. In his parents, I found another father and mother who loved and accepted me as one of their own. His brother and sister treated me like a true sibling. And they loved my grandma too, welcoming her into their circle as naturally as if she had always been part of it. We became a unit, a family stitched together by love.

One year later, Caleb and I sat on the porch, our hands intertwined as autumn leaves whispered across the fields. The evening was perfect, the kind that sticks in your memory long after it's gone, gold fading into indigo, indigo deepening into night. Soon, the heavens opened up, revealing a canopy of glittering stars above us, endless and eternal.

Caleb slipped his hand free of mine. Surprised, I turned toward him. My breath caught. His rugged good looks still made my heart race, but it was more than that. It was his soul, the kindness that shone from his eyes, his love for nature and animals, his steady devotion to people, his fierce love for me. He had spoken those words, "I love you," only months into our relationship, but more importantly, he had lived them every day since. He called to check on me at work. He met me for lunch dates. He danced with me in the wildflower field planted by my dad. He showed me love in every way he knew how.

And I loved him back, in both word and deed. I cooked his favorite meals. I helped with the ranch chores. I stood by him, encouraging him in his work and his dreams. When either of us fell ill or felt weighed down by life, the other was there with comfort, with healing. What began as a friendship had blossomed into something rare, deep, and everlasting.

Caleb's eyes locked on mine, his gaze burning with passion, honesty, and devotion. And then, he fell to his knees. My heart leapt as he drew a small box from his pocket and opened it to reveal a diamond, brilliant and breathtaking, real and true.

"My beautiful Calista," he said, his voice steady, rich with emotion, "will you marry me?" A squeal of joy escaped me before I could stop it. "Yes! Yes, Caleb!" I cried, my laughter and tears mixing as the stars shone down like a thousand blessings. Only later did I learn the secret. Before proposing, Caleb had gone to my grandma to ask for her blessing. He told her that he wished he could ask my dad, and Grandma, with her gentle wisdom, had sent him out to the pasture. "Look up at the sky," she told him. "That's where you'll find him. If the sky smiles down at you, then you'll have his blessing." So Caleb went, and that night, the sky did smile. And now, here beneath the same twinkling stars, I felt Mom and Simon smiling too, our family in heaven joining in the joy of this moment.

We married on the porch, the place where our love had taken root and bloomed under countless sunsets and starlit skies. Friends and family gathered close, not divided into separate sides of a chapel, but joined together in one circle of love, standing on the land that had shaped us both. The scent of wildflowers drifted through the breeze, and the wooden boards beneath our feet seemed to hum with memory, as though the porch itself bore witness to our vows.

When I looked into Caleb's eyes, the world disappeared. I gave myself to him fully, not in fragments, not in cautious pieces, but entirely. My whole heart, my whole life. And he gave himself to me in the same way, steadfast and unreserved. We promised not just to walk side by side but to carry each other when life grew heavy, to laugh when the days were light, to cry when the nights were long.

The stars, though hidden in the bright sky above us, seemed to wait in silence, ready to rise and bless our union. I felt Mom, Dad, and Simon close, smiling from heaven, their love woven into mine. Grandma sat with tears in her eyes, her hands clasped together in joy. Caleb's family, now my family, beamed with pride.

We sealed our vows with a kiss, sweet and sure, and the sound of applause, laughter, and a few happy sobs filled the air. But more than anything, I remember the peace of that moment. The kind of peace that comes when you know you are exactly where you were meant to be, with the person you were always meant to love.

Sometime after that, I learned that Jackie had moved to Europe. Still unmarried, still searching. I often wondered if she would ever find the kind of love that held you steady in the storms of life. I hoped she would. Stephanie and Todd had long since drifted away, their story no longer mine to follow. And as for Daniel, I had nearly forgotten he even existed. He was just a shadow in the distance of my past, a name that carried no weight anymore.

Katie, however, remained a joy in my life. She would call now and then, her voice always full of laughter and light, and our conversations left me smiling long after we hung up. My grandma had grown very frail, and Caleb and I had decided to bring her to the ranch so she could spend her final days wrapped in love and care. I had left my job in town to work beside Caleb, my hands re-learning the thrill of ranch life, my heart at peace with this quieter, truer way of living.

One evening, I sat on the porch breathing in the crisp country air. The pasture was bathed in the golden glow of the setting sun, and I could hear the tractor hum fade into silence as Caleb finished mowing for the day. Grandma was inside, resting before dinner, the casserole bubbling in the oven already filling the air with comfort. The boards of the porch beneath me felt like home, as if they too carried the weight of my story.

I smiled and laid both hands over my belly. A secret lived there, small but mighty, and tonight was the night I would share it. The thought of Caleb's face when I told him made my heart race with joy. A new life was growing inside me, a promise of hope and love renewed.

Lifting my eyes to the sky, streaked in amber and rose, I whispered softly, "Dad, Mom, Simon, this child will carry a piece of each of you. I can already feel it. Thank you for watching over us. I love you, all of you."

That night, after dinner, Caleb and I stepped out onto the porch together. The sky stretched wide and endless above us, the stars beginning to scatter like diamonds across velvet. I leaned into him, my secret still nestled close to my heart, and together we looked upward in silence. Those stars had always carried the memory of my parents and Simon, shining reminders that love never truly leaves us. And now, as they glimmered above our little ranch, I knew they were also lighting the way forward for me, for Caleb, for Grandma, and for the new life stirring within me. Beneath their eternal glow, I felt wrapped in the arms of past, present, and future love.

ABOUT THE AUTHOR

Dana-Susan Crews is an author and childhood cancer advocate. Her greatest passions in life are God, her family, her dog Bella, wildflowers, and a sky full of stars. As a pediatric cancer advocate, she devotes her time to raising awareness and funding to develop better therapies for kids with cancer. You can learn more about her by visiting...

www.ashlandink.com
www.bellasteri.com